William Dean Howells

The Sleeping Car

William Dean Howells

The Sleeping Car

ISBN/EAN: 9783743367531

Manufactured in Europe, USA, Canada, Australia, Japa

Cover: Foto ©Andreas Hilbeck / pixelio.de

Manufactured and distributed by brebook publishing software (www.brebook.com)

William Dean Howells

The Sleeping Car

THE
SLEEPING-CAR

AND

OTHER FARCES

BY

WILLIAM D. HOWELLS

BOSTON AND NEW YORK
HOUGHTON, MIFFLIN AND COMPANY
The Riverside Press, Cambridge

CONTENTS.

THE PARLOR-CAR.

FARCE.

THE PARLOR-CAR.

Farce.

SCENE: A Parlor-Càr on the New York Central Railroad. It is late afternoon in the early autumn, with a cloudy sunset threatening rain. The car is unoccupied save by a gentleman, who sits fronting one of the windows, with his feet in another chair; a newspaper lies across his lap; his hat is drawn down over his eyes, and he is apparently asleep. The rear door of the car opens, and the conductor enters with a young lady, heavily veiled, the porter coming after with her wraps and travelling-bags. The lady's air is of mingled anxiety and desperation, with a certain fierceness of movement. She casts a careless glance over the empty chairs.

Conductor: "Here's your ticket, madam. You can have any of the places you like here, or," — glancing at the unconscious gentleman, and then at the young lady, — "if you prefer, you can go and take that seat in the forward car."

Miss Lucy Galbraith: "Oh, I can't ride backwards. I'll stay here, please. Thank you." The porter places her things in a chair by a window, across the car from the sleeping gentleman, and she throws herself wearily into the next seat, wheels round in it, and lifting her veil gazes absently out at the landscape. Her face, which is very pretty, with a low forehead shadowed by thick blond hair, shows the traces of tears. She makes search in her pocket for her handkerchief, which she presses to her eyes. The conductor, lingering a moment, goes out.

Porter: "I'll be right here, at de end of de cah, if you should happen to want anything, miss," — making a feint of arranging the shawls and satchels. "Should you like some dese things hung up? Well, dey'll be jus' as well in de chair. We's pretty late dis afternoon; more'n four hours behin' time. Ought to been into Albany 'fore dis. Freight train off de track jus' dis side o' Rochester, an' had to wait. Was you going to stop at Schenectady, miss?"

Miss Galbraith, absently: "At Schenectady?" After a pause, "Yes."

Porter: "Well, that's de next station, and den de cahs don't stop ag'in till dey git to Albany. Anything else I can do for you now, miss?"

Miss Galbraith: "No, no, thank you, nothing." The *Porter* hesitates, takes off his cap, and scratches his head with a murmur of embarrassment. *Miss Galbraith* looks up at him inquiringly and then suddenly takes out her porte-monnaie, and fees him.

Porter: "Thank you, miss, thank you. If you want anything at all, miss, I'm right dere at de end of de cah." He goes out by the narrow passage-way beside the smaller enclosed parlor. *Miss Galbraith* looks askance at the sleeping gentleman, and then, rising, goes to the large mirror, to pin her veil, which has become loosened from her hat. She gives a little start at sight of the gentleman in the mirror, but arranges her headgear, and returning to her place looks out of the window again. After a little while she moves about uneasily in her chair, then leans forward, and tries to raise her window; she lifts it partly up, when the catch slips from her fingers, and the window falls shut again with a crash.

Miss Galbraith: "Oh, *dear*, how provoking! I suppose I must call the porter." She rises from her seat, but on attempting to move away she finds that the skirt of her polonaise has been caught in the falling window. She pulls at it, and then tries to lift the window again, but the cloth has wedged it in, and she cannot stir it. "Well, I certainly think this is beyond endurance! Porter! Ah, — Porter! Oh, he'll never hear me in the racket that these wheels are making! I wish they'd stop, — I " — The gentleman stirs in his chair, lifts his head, listens, takes his feet down from the other seat, rises abruptly, and comes to *Miss Galbraith's* side.

Mr. Allen Richards: "Will you allow me to open the window for you?" Starting back, "Miss Galbraith!"

Miss Galbraith: "Al — Mr. Richards!" There is a silence for some moments, in which they remain looking at each other; then, —

Mr. Richards: "Lucy " —

Miss Galbraith: "I forbid you to address me in that way, Mr. Richards."

Mr. Richards: "Why, you were just going to call me Allen!"

Miss Galbraith: "That was an accident, you know very well, — an impulse" —

Mr. Richards: "Well, so is this."

Miss Galbraith: "Of which you ought to be ashamed to take advantage. I wonder at your presumption in speaking to me at all. It's quite idle, I can assure you. Everything is at an end between us. It seems that I bore with you too long; but I'm thankful that I had the spirit to act at last, and to act in time. And now that chance has thrown us together, I trust that you will not force your conversation upon me. No gentleman would, and I have always given you credit for thinking yourself a gentleman. I request that you will not speak to me."

Mr. Richards: "You've spoken ten words to me for every one of mine to you. But I won't annoy you. I can't believe it, Lucy; I can *not* believe it. It seems like some rascally dream, and if I had had any sleep since it happened, I should think I *had* dreamed it."

Miss Galbraith: "Oh! You were sleeping soundly enough when I got into the car!"

Mr. Richards: "I own it; I was perfectly used up, and I *had* dropped off."

Miss Galbraith, scornfully: "Then perhaps you *have* dreamed it."

Mr. Richards: "I'll think so till you tell me again that our engagement is broken; that the faithful love of years is to go for nothing; that you dismiss me with cruel insult, without one word of explanation, without a word of intelligible accusation, even. It's too much! I've been thinking it all over and over, and I can't make head or tail of it. I meant to see you again as soon as we got to town, and implore you to hear me. Come, it's a mighty serious matter, Lucy. I'm not a man to put on heroics and that; but *I* believe it'll play the very deuce with me, Lucy, — that is to say, Miss Galbraith, — I do indeed. It'll give me a low opinion of woman."

Miss Galbraith, averting her face: "Oh, a very high opinion of woman you have had!"

Mr. Richards, with sentiment: "Well, there was one woman whom I thought a perfect angel."

Miss Galbraith: "Indeed! May I ask her name?"

Mr. Richards, with a forlorn smile. "I shall be obliged to describe her somewhat formally as — Miss Galbraith."

Miss Galbraith : " Mr. Richards ! "

Mr. Richards : " Why, you've just forbidden me to say *Lucy!* You must tell me, dearest, what I have done to offend you. The worst criminals are not condemned unheard, and I've always thought you were merciful if not just. And now I only ask you to be just."

Miss Galbraith, looking out of the window : "You know very well what you've done. You can't expect me to humiliate myself by putting your offence into words."

Mr. Richards : " Upon my soul, I don't know what you mean ! I *don't* know what I've done. When you came at me, last night, with my ring and presents and other little traps, you might have knocked me down with the lightest of the lot. I was perfectly dazed ; I couldn't say anything before you were off, and all I could do was to hope that you'd be more like yourself in the morning. And in the morning, when I came round to Mrs. Philips's, I found you were gone, and I came after you by the next train."

Miss Galbraith : "Mr. Richards, your personal history for the last twenty-four hours is a matter of perfect indifference to me, as it shall be for the next twenty-four hundred years. I see that you are resolved to annoy me, and since *you* will not leave the car, *I* must do so." She rises haughtily from her seat, but the imprisoned skirt of her polonaise twitches her abruptly back into her chair. She bursts into tears. "Oh, what *shall* I do ? "

Mr. Richards, dryly : "You shall do whatever you like, Miss Galbraith, when I've set you free; for I see your dress is caught in the window. When it's once out, I'll shut the window, and you can call the porter to raise it." He leans forward over her chair, and while she shrinks back the length of her tether, he tugs at the window-fastening. "I can't get at it. Would you be so good as to stand up, — all you can ? " *Miss Galbraith* stands up, droopingly, and *Mr. Richards* makes a movement towards her, and then falls back. "No, that won't do. Please sit down again." He goes round her chair and tries to get at the window from that side. "I can't get any purchase on it. Why don't you cut out that piece ? " *Miss Galbraith* stares at him in dumb amazement. "Well, I don't see what we're to do. I'll go and get the porter." He goes to the end of the car, and returns. " I can't find the porter, — he must be in one of the other cars. But " — brightening with the fortunate conception — " I've just thought of something. Will it unbutton ? "

Miss Galbraith : " Unbutton ? "

Mr. Richards : " Yes ; this garment of yours."

Miss Galbraith : " My polonaise ? " Inquiringly, " Yes."

Mr. Richards : " Well, then, it's a very simple matter. If you will just take it off I can easily " —

Miss Galbraith, faintly : " I can't. A polonaise isn't like an *overcoat* " —

Mr. Richards, with dismay : " Oh ! Well, then " — He remains thinking a moment in hopeless perplexity.

Miss Galbraith, with polite ceremony : " The porter will be back soon. Don't trouble yourself any further about it, please. I shall do very well."

Mr. Richards, without heeding her : " If you could kneel on that foot-cushion, and face the window " —

Miss Galbraith, kneeling promptly : " So ? "

Mr. Richards : " Yes, and now " — kneeling beside her — "if you'll allow me to — to get at the window-catch," — he stretches both arms forward; she shrinks from his right into his left, and then back again, — "and pull, while I raise the window " —

Miss Galbraith: "Yes, yes; but do hurry, please. If any one saw us, I don't know what they would think. It's perfectly ridiculous!" — pulling. " It's caught in the corner of the window, between the frame and the sash, and it won't come! Is my hair troubling you? Is it in your eyes? "

Mr. Richards: "It's in my eyes, but it isn't troubling me. Am I inconveniencing you?"

Miss Galbraith: "Oh, not at all."

Mr. Richards: "Well, now then, pull hard!" He lifts the window with a great effort; the polonaise comes free with a start, and she strikes violently against him. In supporting the shock he cannot forbear catching her for an instant to his heart. She frees herself, and starts indignantly to her feet.

Miss Galbraith: "Oh, what a cowardly — subterfuge!"

Mr. Richards: "Cowardly? You've no idea

how much courage it took." *Miss Galbraith* puts her handkerchief to her face, and sobs. "Oh, don't cry! Bless my heart, — I'm sorry I did it! But you know how dearly I love you, Lucy, though I do think you've been cruelly unjust. I told you I never should love any one else, and I never shall. I couldn't help it; upon my soul, I couldn't. Nobody could. Don't let it vex you, my" — He approaches her.

Miss Galbraith: "Please not touch me, sir! You have no longer any right whatever to do so."

Mr. Richards: "You misinterpret a very inoffensive gesture. I have no idea of touching you, but I hope I may be allowed, as a special favor, to — pick up my hat, which you are in the act of stepping on." *Miss Galbraith* hastily turns, and strikes the hat with her whirling skirts; it rolls to the other side of the parlor, and *Mr. Richards*, who goes after it, utters an ironical "Thanks!" He brushes it, and puts it on, looking at her where she has again seated herself at the window with her back to him, and continues, "As for any further molestation from me" —

Miss Galbraith: "If you *will* talk to me" —

Mr. Richards: "Excuse me, I am not talking to you."

Miss Galbraith: "What were you doing?"

Mr. Richards: "I was beginning to think aloud. I — I was soliloquizing. I suppose I may be allowed to soliloquize?"

Miss Galbraith, very coldly: "You can do what you like."

Mr. Richards: "Unfortunately that's just what I can't do. If I could do as I liked, I should ask you a single question."

Miss Galbraith, after a moment: "Well, sir, you may ask your question." She remains as before, with her chin in her hand, looking tearfully out of the window; her face is turned from *Mr. Richards,* who hesitates a moment before he speaks.

Mr. Richards: "I wish to ask you just this, Miss Galbraith: if you couldn't ride backwards in the other car, why do you ride backwards in this?"

Miss Galbraith, burying her face in her hand-kerchief, and sobbing: "Oh, oh, oh! This is too bad!"

Mr. Richards: "Oh, come now, Lucy. It breaks my heart to hear you going on so, and all for nothing. Be a little merciful to both of us, and listen to me. I've no doubt I can explain everything if I once understand it, but it's pretty hard explaining a thing if you don't understand it yourself. Do turn round. I know it makes you sick to ride in that way, and if you don't want to face me — there ! " — wheeling in his chair so as to turn his back upon her — " you needn't. Though it's rather trying to a fellow's politeness, not to mention his other feelings. Now, what in the name " —

Porter, who at this moment enters with his step-ladder, and begins to light the lamps : " Going pretty slow ag'in, sah."

Mr. Richards : " Yes ; what's the trouble ? "

Porter : " Well, I don't know exactly, sah. Something de matter with de locomotive. We sha'n't be into Albany much 'fore eight o'clock."

Mr. Richards : " What's the next station ? "

Porter : " Schenectady."

Mr. Richards : " Is the whole train as empty as this car ? "

Porter, laughing : " Well, no, sah. Fact is, *dis* cah don't belong on dis train. It's a Pullman that we hitched on when you got in, and we's taking it along for one of de Eastern roads. We let you in 'cause de Drawing-rooms was all full. Same with de lady," — looking sympathetically at her, as he takes his steps to go out. "Can I do anything for you now, miss ?"

Miss Galbraith, plaintively: "No, thank you; nothing whatever." She has turned while *Mr. Richards* and *The Porter* have been speaking, and now faces the back of the former, but her veil is drawn closely. *The Porter* goes out.

Mr. Richards, wheeling round so as to confront her: "I wish you would speak to me half as kindly as you do to that darky, Lucy."

Miss Galbraith : " He is a gentleman ! "

Mr. Richards: "He is an urbane and well-informed nobleman. At any rate, he's a man and a brother. But so am I." *Miss Galbraith* does not reply, and after a pause *Mr. Richards* resumes. "Talking of gentlemen, I recollect, once, coming up on the day-boat to Poughkeepsie, there was a poor devil of a tipsy man kept following a young fellow about, and annoying him to death — trying to fight him, as a tipsy man will, and insisting that the young fellow had insulted him. By and by he lost his balance and went overboard, and the other

jumped after him and fished him out." Sensation
on the part of *Miss Galbraith*, who stirs uneasily
in her chair, looks out of the window, then looks
at *Mr. Richards*, and drops her head. "There was
a young lady on board, who had seen the whole
thing — a very charming young lady indeed, with
pale-blond hair growing very thick over her forehead, and dark eyelashes to the sweetest blue eyes
in the world. Well, this young lady's papa was
amongst those who came up to say civil things to
the young fellow when he got aboard again, and to
ask the honor — he said the *honor* — of his acquaintance. And when he came out of his state-
room in dry clothes, this infatuated old gentleman
was waiting for him, and took him and introduced
him to his wife and daughter; and the daughter
said, with tears in her eyes, and a perfectly intoxi-
cating impulsiveness, that it was the grandest and
the most heroic and the noblest thing that she had
ever seen, and she should always be a better girl
for having seen it. Excuse me, Miss Galbraith,
for troubling you with these facts of a personal
history, which, as you say, is a matter of perfect
indifference to you. The young fellow didn't
think at the time he had done anything extraor-

dinary; but I don't suppose he *did* expect to live
to have the same girl tell him he was no gentleman."

Miss Galbraith, wildly: "O Allen, Allen! You
know I think you are a gentleman, and I always
did!"

Mr. Richards, languidly: "Oh, I merely. had
your word for it, just now, that you didn't."
Tenderly, "Will you hear me, Lucy?"

Miss Galbraith, faintly: "Yes."

Mr. Richards: "Well, what is it I've done?
Will you tell me if I guess right?"

Miss Galbraith, with dignity: "I am in no
humor for jesting, Allen. And I can assure you
that though I consent to hear what you have to
say, or ask, *nothing* will change my determination.
All is over between us."

Mr. Richards: "Yes, I understand that, perfectly. I am now asking merely for general in-
formation. I do not expect you to relent, and,
in fact, I should consider it rather frivolous if you
did. No. What I have always admired in your
character, Lucy, is a firm, logical consistency; a
clearness of mental vision that leaves no side of
a subject unsearched; and an unwavering con-

stancy of purpose. You may say that these traits are characteristic of *all* women; but they are pre-eminently characteristic of you, Lucy." *Miss Galbraith* looks askance at him, to make out whether he is in earnest or not; he continues, with a perfectly serious air. "And I know now that if you're offended with me, it's for no trivial cause." She stirs uncomfortably in her chair. "What I have done I can't imagine, but it must be something monstrous, since it has made life with me appear so impossible that you are ready to fling away your own happiness — for I know you *did* love me, Lucy — and destroy mine. I will begin with the worst thing I can think of. Was it be-cause I danced so much with Fanny Watervliet?"

Miss Galbraith, indignantly: "How can you insult me by supposing that I could be jealous of such a *perfect* little goose as that? No, Allen! Whatever I think of you, I *still* respect you too much for *that*."

Mr. Richards: "I'm glad to hear that there are yet depths to which you think me incapable of descending, and that Miss Watervliet is one of them. I will now take a little higher ground. Perhaps you think I flirted with Mrs. Dawes. I thought, myself, that the thing might begin to have that appearance, but I give you my word of honor that as soon as the idea occurred to me, I dropped her — rather rudely, too. The trouble was, don't you know, that I felt so perfectly safe with a *married* friend of yours. I couldn't be hanging about you all the time, and I was afraid I might vex you if I went with the other girls; and I didn't know what to do."

Miss Galbraith: "I think you behaved rather silly, giggling so much with her. But" —

Mr. Richards: "I own it, I know it was silly. But" —

Miss Galbraith: "It wasn't that; it wasn't that!"

Mr. Richards: "Was it my forgetting to bring you those things from your mother?"

Miss Galbraith: "No!"

Mr. Richards: "Was it because I hadn't given up smoking yet?"

Miss Galbraith: "You *know* I never asked you to give up smoking. It was entirely your own proposition."

Mr. Richards: "That's true. That's what made me so easy about it. I knew I could leave it off *any* time. Well, I will not disturb you any longer, Miss Galbraith." He throws his overcoat across his arm, and takes up his travelling-bag. " I have failed to guess your fatal — conundrum ; and I have no longer any excuse for remaining. I am going into the smoking-car. Shall I send the porter to you for anything ? "

Miss Galbraith : " No, thanks." She puts up her handkerchief to her face.

Mr. Richards : " Lucy, do you send me away ? "

Miss Galbraith, behind her handkerchief : " You were going, yourself."

Mr. Richards, over his shoulder : " Shall I come back ? "

Miss Galbraith : " I have no right to drive you from the car."

Mr. Richards, coming back, and sitting down in the chair nearest her : " Lucy, dearest, tell me what's the matter."

Miss Galbraith : " O Allen ! your not *knowing* makes it all the more hopeless and killing. It shows me that we *must* part ; that you would go on, breaking my heart, and grinding me into the dust as long as we lived." She sobs. " It shows me that you never understood me, and you never will. I know you're good and kind and all that, but that only makes your not understanding me so much the worse. I do it quite as much for your sake as my own, Allen."

Mr. Richards: "I'd much rather you wouldn't put yourself out on my account."

Miss Galbraith, without regarding him: "If you could mortify me before a whole roomful of people, as you did last night, what could I expect after marriage but continual insult?"

Mr. Richards, in amazement: "*How* did I mortify you? I thought that I treated you with all the tenderness and affection that a decent regard for the feelings of others would allow. I was ashamed to find I couldn't keep away from you."

Miss Galbraith: "Oh, you were *attentive* enough, Allen; nobody denies that. Attentive enough in non-essentials. Oh, yes!"

Mr. Richards: "Well, what vital matters did I fail in? I'm sure I can't remember."

Miss Galbraith: "I dare say! I dare say they won't appear vital to you, Allen. Nothing does. And if I had told you, I should have been met with ridicule, I suppose. But I knew *better* than to tell; I respected myself too *much.*"

Mr. Richards : "But now you mustn't respect yourself *quite* so much, dearest. And I promise you I won't laugh at the most serious thing. I'm in no humor for it. If it were a matter of life and death, even, I can assure you that it wouldn't bring a smile to my countenance. No, indeed! If you expect me to laugh, *now*, you must say something particularly funny."

Miss Galbraith : "I was not going to say anything *funny*, as you call it, and I will say nothing at all, if you talk in that way."

Mr. Richards : "Well, I won't, then. But do you know what I suspect, Lucy? I wouldn't mention it to everybody, but I will to you — in strict confidence : I suspect that you're rather ashamed of your grievance, if you have any. I suspect it's nothing at all."

Miss Galbraith, very sternly at first, with a rising hysterical inflection : "Nothing, Allen! Do you call it *nothing*, to have Mrs. Dawes come out with all that about your accident on your way up the river, and ask me if it didn't frighten me terribly to hear of it, even after it was all over; and I had to say you hadn't told me a word of it? 'Why, Lucy!'" — angrily mimicking Mrs. Dawes,

—" 'you must teach him better than that. I make Mr. Dawes tell *me* everything.' Little simpleton! And then to have them all laugh — Oh, dear, it's too much!"

Mr. Richards: "Why, my dear Lucy"—

Miss Galbraith, interrupting him: "I saw just how it was going to be, and I'm thankful, *thankful* that it happened. I saw that you didn't care enough for me to take me into your whole life; that you despised and distrusted me, and that it would get worse and worse to the end of our days; that we should grow farther and farther apart, and I should be left moping at home, while you ran about making confidantes of other women whom you considered *worthy* of your confidence. It all *flashed* upon me in an *instant;* and I resolved to break with you, then and there; and I did, just as soon as ever I could go to my room for your things, and I'm glad, — yes, — Oh, hu, hu, hu, hu, hu! — *so* glad I did it!"

Mr. Richards, grimly: "Your joy is obvious. May I ask"—

Miss Galbraith: "Oh, it wasn't the *first* proof you had given me how little you really cared for me, but I was determined it should be the last. I dare say you've forgotten them! I dare say you don't remember telling Mamie Morris that you didn't like embroidered cigar-cases, when you'd just *told* me that you did, and let me be such a fool as to commence one for you; but I'm thankful to say *that* went into the fire, — oh, yes, *instantly!* And I dare say you've forgotten that you didn't tell me your brother's engagement was to be kept, and let me come out with it that night at the Rudges', and then looked perfectly aghast, so that everybody thought I had been blabbing! Time and again, Allen, you have made me suffer agonies, yes, *agonies ;* but your power to do so is at an end. I am free and happy at last." She weeps bitterly.

Mr. Richards, quietly: "Yes, I *had* forgotten those crimes, and I suppose many similar atrocities. I own it, I *am* forgetful and careless. I was wrong about those things. I ought to have told you why I said that to Miss Morris : I was afraid she was going to work me one. As to that accident I told Mrs. Dawes of, it wasn't worth mentioning. Our boat simply walked over a sloop in the night, and nobody was hurt. I shouldn't have thought twice about it, if she hadn't happened to brag of their passing close to an iceberg on their way home from Europe; then I trotted out *my* pretty-near disaster as a match for hers, — confound her! I wish the iceberg had sunk them! Only it wouldn't have sunk her, — she's so light; she'd have gone bobbing about all over the Atlantic Ocean, like a cork; she's got a perfect life-preserver in that mind of hers." *Miss Galbraith* gives a little laugh, and then a little moan. "But since you are happy, I will not repine, Miss Galbraith. I don't pretend to be very happy myself, but then, I don't deserve it. Since you are ready to let an absolutely unconscious offence on my part cancel all the past; since you let my devoted love weigh as nothing against the momentary pique that a malicious little rattle-pate — she was vexed at my leaving her — could make you feel, and choose to gratify a wicked resentment at the cost of any suffering to me, why, *I* can be glad and happy too." With rising anger, " Yes, Miss Galbraith. All *is* over between us. You can go! I renounce you!"

Miss Galbraith, springing fiercely to her feet: "Go, indeed! Renounce me! Be so good as to remember that you haven't got me *to* renounce!"

Mr. Richards: " Well, it's all the same thing.

I'd renounce you if I had. Good-evening, Miss
Galbraith. I will send back your presents as soon
as I get to town; it won't be necessary to acknowledge them. I hope we may never meet again."
He goes out of the door towards the front of the
car, but returns directly, and glances uneasily at
Miss Galbraith, who remains with her handkerchief pressed to her eyes. "Ah — a — that is —
I shall be obliged to intrude upon you again. The
fact is " —

Miss Galbraith, anxiously : " Why, the cars have
stopped! Are we at Schenectady ? "

Mr. Richards : "Well, no; not *exactly ;* not
exactly at *Schenectady*" —

Miss Galbraith : " Then what station is this ?
Have they carried me by ? " Observing his embarrassment, " Allen, what is the matter ? What
has happened ? Tell me instantly ! Are we off
the track ? Have we run into another train ?
Have we broken through a bridge ? Shall we be
burnt alive ? Tell me, Allen, tell me, — I can bear
it ! — are we telescoped ? " She wrings her hands
in terror.

Mr. Richards, unsympathetically : "Nothing of
the kind has happened. This car has simply come

uncoupled, and the rest of the train has gone on ahead, and left us standing on the track, nowhere in particular." He leans back in his chair, and wheels it round from her.

Miss Galbraith, mortified, yet anxious : " Well ? "

Mr. Richards : " Well, until they miss us, and run back to pick us up, I shall be obliged to ask your indulgence. I will try not to disturb you; I would go out and stand on the platform, but it's raining."

Miss Galbraith, listening to the rain-fall on the roof : " Why, so it is ! " Timidly, " Did you notice when the car stopped ? "

Mr. Richards : " No." He rises and goes out at the rear door, comes back, and sits down again.

Miss Galbraith, rises, and goes to the large mirror to wipe away her tears. She glances at *Mr. Richards,* who does not move. She sits down in a seat nearer him than the chair she has left. After some faint murmurs and hesitations, she asks, " Will you please tell me why you went out just now ? "

Mr. Richards, with indifference : " Yes. I went to see if the rear signal was out."

Miss Galbraith, after another hesitation: " Why ? "

Mr. Richards : " Because, if it wasn't out, some train might run into us from that direction."

Miss Galbraith, tremulously : "Oh ! And was it ?"

Mr. Richards, dryly : " Yes."

Miss Galbraith returns to her former place, with a wounded air, and for a moment neither speaks. Finally she asks very meekly, " And there's no danger from the front ? "

Mr. Richards, coldly : " No."

Miss Galbraith, after some little noises and movements meant to catch *Mr. Richards's* attention: " Of course, I never meant to imply that you were *intentionally* careless or forgetful."

Mr. Richards, still very coldly : " Thank you."

Miss Galbraith : " I always did justice to your good-heartedness, Allen ; you're perfectly lovely that way ; and I know that you would be sorry if you *knew* you had wounded my feelings, however accidentally." She droops her head so as to catch a sidelong glimpse of his face, and sighs, while she nervously pinches the top of her parasol, resting the point on the floor. *Mr. Richards* makes no answer. " That about the cigar-case might have been a mistake; I saw that myself, and, as you explain it, why, it was certainly very kind and very creditable to — to your thoughtfulness. It *was* thoughtful!"

Mr. Richards: "I am grateful for your good opinion."

Miss Galbraith: "But do you think it was exactly — it was quite — nice, not to tell me that your brother's engagement was to be kept, when you know, Allen, I can't bear to blunder in such things?" Tenderly, "*Do* you? You *can't* say it was?"

Mr. Richards: "I never said it was."

Miss Galbraith, plaintively: "No, Allen. That's what I always admired in your character. You always owned up. Don't you think it's easier for men to own up than it is for women?"

Mr. Richards: "I don't know. I never knew any woman to do it."

Miss Galbraith: "Oh, yes, Allen! You know I *often* own up."

Mr. Richards: "No, I don't."

Miss Galbraith: "Oh, how can you bear to say so? When I'm rash, or anything of that kind, you know I acknowledge it."

Mr. Richards : "Do you acknowledge it now ?"

Miss Galbraith : "Why, how can I, when I haven't *been* rash? *What* have I been rash about ? "

Mr. Richards : "About the cigar-case, for example."

Miss Galbraith : "Oh! *that!* That was a great while ago! I thought you meant something quite recent." A sound as of the approaching train is heard in the distance. She gives a start, and then leaves her chair again for one a little nearer his. "I thought perhaps you meant about — last night."

Mr. Richards : "Well."

Miss Galbraith, very judicially : "I don't think it was *rash*, exactly. No, not *rash*. It might not have been very *kind* not to — to — trust you more, when I knew that you didn't mean anything; but — No, I took the only course I could. *Nobody* could have done differently under the circumstances. But if I caused you any pain, I 'm very sorry; oh, yes, very sorry indeed. But I was not precipitate, and I know I did right. At least I *tried* to act for the best. Don't you believe I did ? "

Mr. Richards: "Why, if you have no doubt upon the subject, my opinion is of no consequence."

Miss Galbraith: "Yes. But what do you think? If you think differently, and can make me see it differently, oughtn't you to do so?"

Mr. Richards: "I don't see why. As you say, all is over between us."   ·

Miss Galbraith: "Yes." After a pause, "I should suppose you would care enough for *yourself* to wish me to look at the matter from the right point of view."

Mr. Richards: "I don't."

Miss Galbraith, becoming more and more uneasy as the noise of the approaching train grows louder: "I think *you* have been very quick with *me* at times, quite as quick as I could have been with you last night." The noise is more distinctly heard. "I'm sure that if I could once see it as you do, *no* one would be more willing to do anything in their power to atone for their rashness. Of course I know that everything is over."

Mr. Richards: "As to that, I have your word; and, in view of the fact, perhaps this analysis of motive, of character, however interesting on general grounds, is a little " —

Miss Galbraith, with sudden violence: " Say it, and take your revenge! I have put myself at your feet, and you do right to trample on me! Oh, this is what women may expect when they trust to men's generosity! Well, it *is* over now, and I'm thankful, thankful! Cruel, suspicious, vindictive, you're all alike, and I'm glad that I'm no longer subject to your heartless caprices. And I don't care what happens after this, I shall always — Oh! You're sure it's from the front, Allen? Are you sure the rear signal is out? "

Mr. Richards, relenting: " Yes, but if it will ease your mind, I'll go and look again." He rises, and starts towards the rear door.

Miss Galbraith, quickly: " Oh, no! Don't go! I can't bear to be left alone!" The sound of the approaching train continually increases in volume. " Oh, isn't it coming very, very, *very* fast? "

Mr. Richards: " No, no! Don't be frightened."

Miss Galbraith, running towards the rear door. " Oh, I *must* get out! It will kill me, I know it will. Come with me! Do, do!" He runs after her, and her voice is heard at the rear of the car.

"Oh, the outside door is locked, and we are trapped, trapped, trapped! Oh, quick! Let's try the door at the other end." They re-enter the parlor, and the roar of the train announces that it is upon them. "No, no! It's too late, it's too late! I'm a wicked, wicked girl, and this is all to punish me! Oh, it's coming, it's coming at full speed!" He remains bewildered, confronting her. She utters a wild cry, and as the train strikes the car with a violent concussion, she flings herself into his arms. "There, there! Forgive me, Allen! Let us die together, my own, own love!" She hangs fainting on his breast. Voices are heard without, and after a little delay *The Porter* comes in with a lantern.

Porter: "Rather more of a jah than we meant to give you, sah! We had to run down pretty quick after we missed you, and the rain made the track a little slippery. Lady much frightened?"

Miss Galbraith, disengaging herself: "Oh, not at all! Not in the least. We thought it was a train coming from behind, and going to run into us, and so — we — I " —

Porter: "Not quite so bad as that. We'll be into Schenectady in a few minutes, miss. I'll come for your things." He goes out at the other door.

Miss Galbraith, in a fearful whisper: "Allen! What will he ever think of us? I'm sure he saw us!"

Mr. Richards: "I don't know what he'll think *now*. He *did* think you were frightened; but you told him you were not. However, it isn't important what he thinks. Probably he thinks I'm your long-lost brother. It had a kind of family look."

Miss Galbraith: "Ridiculous!"

Mr. Richards: "Why, he'd never suppose that I was a jilted lover of yours!"

Miss Galbraith, ruefully: "No."

Mr. Richards: "Come, Lucy,"—taking her hand,—"you wished to die with me, a moment ago. Don't you think you can make one more effort to live with me? I won't take advantage of words spoken in mortal peril, but I suppose you were in earnest when you called me your own —own "— Her head droops; he folds her in his arms a moment, then she starts away from him, as if something had suddenly occurred to her.

Miss Galbraith: "Allen, where are you going?"

Mr. Richards: "Going? Upon my soul, I haven't the least idea."

Miss Galbraith: "Where *were* you going?"

Mr. Richards: "Oh, I *was* going to Albany."

Miss Galbraith: "Well, don't! Aunt Mary is expecting me here at Schenectady, — I telegraphed her, — and I want you to stop here, too, and we'll refer the whole matter to her. She's such a wise old head. I'm not sure" —

Mr. Richards: "What?"

Miss Galbraith, demurely: "That I'm good enough for you."

Mr. Richards, starting, in burlesque of her move- ment, as if a thought had struck *him:* "Lucy! how came you on this train when you left Syracuse on the morning express?"

Miss Galbraith, faintly: "I waited over a train at Utica." She sinks into a chair, and averts her face.

Mr. Richards: "May I ask why?"

Miss Galbraith, more faintly still: "I don't like to tell. I" —

Mr. Richards, coming and standing in front of her, with his hands in his pockets: "Look me in the eye, Lucy!" She drops her veil over her face, and looks up at him. "Did you — did you expect to find *me* on this train ? "

Miss Galbraith : "I was afraid it never *would* get along, — it was so late ! "

Mr. Richards : "Don't — tergiversate."

Miss Galbraith : "Don't *what ?* "

Mr. Richards : " Fib."

Miss Galbraith : "Not for worlds ! "

Mr. Richards : "How did you know I was in this car ? "

Miss Galbraith : "Must I ? I thought I saw you through the window; and then I made sure it was you when I went to pin my veil on, — I saw you in the mirror."

Mr. Richards, after a little silence : "Miss Galbraith, do you want to know what *you* are ? "

Miss Galbraith, softly : "Yes, Allen."

Mr. Richards : "You're a humbug ! "

Miss Galbraith, springing from her seat, and confronting him. "So are you ! You pretended to be asleep ! "

Mr. Richards : "I — I — I was taken by surprise. I had to take time to think."

Miss Galbraith : "So did I."

Mr. Richards: "And you thought it would be a good plan to get your polonaise caught in the window?"

Miss Galbraith, hiding her face on his shoulder: "No, no, Allen! That I never *will* admit. *No* woman would!"

Mr. Richards: "Oh, I dare say!" After a pause: "Well, I am a poor, weak, helpless man, with no one to advise me or counsel me, and I have been cruelly deceived. How could you, Lucy, how could you? I can never get over this." He drops his head upon her shoulder.

Miss Galbraith, starting away again, and looking about the car: "Allen, I have an idea! Do you suppose Mr. Pullman could be induced to *sell* this car?"

Mr. Richards: "Why?"

Miss Galbraith: "Why, because I think it's perfectly lovely, and I should like to live in it always. It could be fitted up for a sort of summer-house, don't you know, and we could have it in the garden, and you could smoke in it."

Mr. Richards: "Admirable! It would look just like a travelling photographic saloon. No, Lucy, we won't buy it; we will simply keep it

as a precious souvenir, a sacred memory, a beautiful dream, — and let it go on fulfilling its destiny all the same."

Porter, entering, and gathering up *Miss Galbraith's* things: "Be at Schenectady in half a minute, miss. Won't have much time."

Miss Galbraith, rising, and adjusting her dress, and then looking about the car, while she passes her hand through her lover's arm: "Oh, I do *hate* to leave it. Farewell, you dear, kind, good, lovely car! May you never have another accident!" She kisses her hand to the car, upon which they both look back as they slowly leave it.

Mr. Richards, kissing his hand in the like manner: "Good-by, sweet chariot! May you never carry any but bridal couples!"

Miss Galbraith: "Or engaged ones!"

Mr. Richards: "Or husbands going home to their wives!"

Miss Galbraith: "Or wives hastening to their husbands."

Mr. Richards: "Or young ladies who have waited one train over, so as to be with the young men they hate."

Miss Galbraith : "Or young men who are so indifferent that they pretend to be asleep when the young ladies come in !" They pause at the door and look back again. " 'And must I leave thee, Paradise ? ' " They both kiss their hands to the car again, and, their faces being very close together, they impulsively kiss each other. Then *Miss Galbraith* throws back her head, and solemnly confronts him. "Only think, Allen ! If this car hadn't broken *its* engagement, we might never have mended ours."

THE SLEEPING-CAR.

FARCE.

THE SLEEPING-CAR.

𝔉𝔞𝔯𝔠𝔢.

I.

Scene: One side of a sleeping-car on the Boston
and Albany Road. The curtains are drawn
before most of the berths: from the hooks and
rods hang hats, bonnets, bags, bandboxes, um-
brellas, and other travelling-gear; on the floor
are boots of both sexes, set out for *The Porter*
to black. *The Porter* is making up the beds in
the upper and lower berths adjoining the seats
on which a young mother, slender and pretty,
with a baby asleep on the seat beside her, and a
stout old lady, sit confronting each other — *Mrs.
Agnes Roberts* and her *Aunt Mary.*

Mrs. Roberts: "Do you always take down your
back hair, aunty?"

Aunt Mary: "No, never, child; at least not
since I had such a fright about it once, coming on
from New York. It's all well enough to take

down your back hair if it *is* yours; but if it isn't, your head's the best place for it. Now, as I buy mine of Madame Pierrot" —

Mrs. Roberts: "Don't you *wish* she wouldn't advertise it as *human* hair? It sounds so pokerish — like human flesh, you know."

Aunt Mary: "Why, she couldn't call it *in*human hair, my dear."

Mrs. Roberts, thoughtfully: "No — just *hair.*"

Aunt Mary: "Then people might think it was for mattresses. But, as I was saying, I took it off that night, and tucked it safely away, as I supposed, in my pocket, and I slept sweetly till about midnight, when I happened to open my eyes, and saw something long and black crawl off my bed and slip under the berth. *Such* a shriek as I gave, my dear! 'A snake! a snake! oh, a snake!' And everybody began talking at once, and some of the gentlemen swearing, and the porter came running with the poker to kill it; and all the while it was that ridiculous switch of mine, that had worked out of my pocket. And glad enough I was to grab it up before anybody saw it, and say I must have been dreaming."

Mrs. Roberts: "Why, aunty, how funny! How

could you suppose a serpent could get on board a sleeping-car, of all places in the world ? "

Aunt Mary : " That was the perfect absurdity of it."

The Porter : " Berths ready now, ladies."

Mrs. Roberts, to *The Porter,* who walks away to the end of the car, and sits down near the door : " Oh, thank you ! — Aunty, do you feel nervous the least bit ? "

Aunt Mary : " Nervous ? No. Why ? "

Mrs. Roberts : " Well, I don't know. I suppose I've been worked up a little about meeting Willis, and wondering how he'll look, and all. We can't *know* each other, of course. It doesn't stand to reason that if he's been out there for twelve years, ever since I was a child, though we've corresponded regularly — at least *I* have — that he could recognize me; not at the first glance, you know. He'll have a full beard; and then I've got married, and here's the baby. Oh, *no !* he'll never guess who it is in the world. Photographs really amount to nothing in such a case. I wish we were at home, and it was all over. I wish he had written some particulars, instead of telegraphing from Ogden, ' Be with you on the 7 A.M., Wednesday.' "

Aunt Mary: "Californians always telegraph, my dear; they never think of writing. It isn't expensive enough, and it doesn't make your blood run cold enough, to get a letter, and so they send you one of those miserable yellow despatches whenever they can — those printed in a long string, if possible, so that you'll be *sure* to die before you get to the end of it. I suppose your brother has fallen into all those ways, and says 'reckon' and 'ornary' and 'which the same,' just like one of Mr. Bret Harte's characters."

Mrs. Roberts: "But it isn't exactly our not knowing each other, aunty, that's worrying me; that's something that could be got over in time. What is simply driving me distracted is Willis and Edward meeting there when I'm away from home. Oh, how *could* I be away! and why *couldn't* Willis have given us fair warning? I would have hurried from the ends of the earth to meet him. I don't believe poor Edward ever saw a Californian; and he's so quiet and pre-occupied, I'm sure he'd never get on with Willis. And if Willis is the least loud, he wouldn't like Edward. Not that I suppose he *is* loud; but I don't believe he knows anything about literary men. But you can see,

aunty, can't you, how very anxious I must be ?
Don't you see that I ought to have been there
when Willis and Edward met, so as to — to — well,
to *break* them to each other, don't you know ? "

Aunt Mary: "Oh, you needn't be troubled
about that, Agnes. I dare say they've got on
perfectly well together. Very likely they're sitting down to the unwholesomest hot supper this
instant that the ingenuity of man could invent."

Mrs. Roberts: "Oh, do you *think* they are,
aunty ? Oh, if I could *only* believe they were
sitting down to a hot supper together now, I should
be *so* happy ! They'd be sure to get on if they
were. There's nothing like eating to make men
friendly with each other. Don't you know, at
receptions, how they never have anything to say
to each other till the escalloped oysters and the
chicken salad appear; and then how sweet they
are as soon as they've helped the ladies to ice ?
Oh, thank you, *thank* you, aunty, for thinking of
the hot supper ! It's such a relief to my mind !
You can understand, can't you, aunty dear, how
anxious I must have been to have my only brother
and my only — my husband — get on nicely together ? My life would be a wreck, simply a

wreck, if they didn't. And Willis and I not having seen each other since I was a child makes it all the worse. I do *hope* they're sitting down to a hot supper."

An angry Voice from the next berth but one: "I wish people in sleeping-cars" —

A Voice from the berth beyond that: "You're mistaken in your premises, sir. This is a waking-car. Ladies, go on, and oblige an eager listener." Sensation, and smothered laughter from the other berths.

Mrs. Roberts, after a space of terrified silence, in a loud whisper to her *Aunt:* "What horrid things! But now we really must go to bed. It *was* too bad to keep talking. I'd no idea my voice was getting so loud. Which berth will you have, aunty? I'd better take the upper one, because" —

Aunt Mary, whispering: "No, no; I must take that, so that you can be with the baby below."

Mrs. Roberts: "Oh, how good you are, Aunt Mary! It's too bad; it is really. I can't let you."

Aunt Mary: "Well, then, you must; that's all. You know how that child tosses and kicks about in the night. You never can tell where his head's going to be in the morning, but you'll probably find it at the foot of the bed. I couldn't sleep an instant, my dear, if I thought that boy was in the upper berth; for I'd be sure of his tumbling out over you. Here, let me lay him down." She lays the baby in the lower berth. "There! Now get in, Agnes — do, and leave me to my struggle with the attraction of gravitation."

Mrs. Roberts: "Oh, *poor* aunty, how will you ever manage it? I *must* help you up."

Aunt Mary: "No, my dear; don't be foolish. But you may go and call the porter, if you like. I dare say he's used to it."

Mrs. Roberts goes and speaks timidly to *The Porter,* who fails at first to understand, then smiles broadly, accepts a quarter with a duck of his head, and comes forward to *Aunt Mary's* side: "Had he better give you his hand to rest your foot in, while you spring up as if you were mounting horseback?"

Aunt Mary, with disdain: "*Spring!* My dear, I haven't *sprung* for a quarter of a century. I shall require every fibre in the man's body. His hand, indeed! You get in first, Agnes."

Mrs. Roberts: "I will, aunty dear; but" —

Aunt Mary, sternly: "Agnes, do as I say."
Mrs. Roberts crouches down on the lower berth.
"I don't choose that any member of my family
shall witness my contortions. Don't you look."

Mrs. Roberts: "No, no, aunty."

Aunt Mary: "Now, porter, are you strong?"

Porter: "I used to be porter at a Saratoga hotel,
and carried up de ladies' trunks dere."

Aunt Mary: "Then you'll do, I think. Now,
then, your knee; now your back. There! And
very handsomely done; thanks."

Mrs. Roberts: "Are you really in, Aunt Mary?"

Aunt Mary, dryly: "Yes. Good-night."

Mrs. Roberts: "Good-night, aunty." After a
pause of some minutes. "Aunty!"

Aunt Mary: "Well, what?"

Mrs. Roberts: "Do you think it's perfectly
safe?" She rises in her berth, and looks up over
the edge of the upper.

Aunt Mary: "I suppose so. It's a well-managed
road. They've got the air-brake, I've heard, and
the Miller platform, and all those horrid things.
What makes you introduce such unpleasant sub-
jects?"

Mrs. Roberts: "Oh, I don't mean accidents. But,

you know, when you turn, it does creak so awfully.
I shouldn't mind myself; but the baby " —

Aunt Mary: "Why, child, do you think I'm
going to break through? I couldn't. I'm one of
the *lightest* sleepers in the world."

Mrs. Roberts: "Yes, I know you're a light
sleeper; but — but it doesn't seem quite the same
thing, somehow."

Aunt Mary: "But it is; it's quite the same
thing, and you can be perfectly easy in your mind,
my dear. I should be quite as loath to break
through as you would to have me. Good-night."

Mrs. Roberts: "Yes; good-night. — Aunty!"

Aunt Mary: "Well?"

Mrs. Roberts: "You ought to just see him,
how he's lying. He's a perfect log. *Couldn't* you
just bend over, and peep down at him a moment?"

Aunt Mary: "Bend over! It would be the
death of me. Good-night."

Mrs. Roberts: "Good-night. Did you put the
glass into my bag, or yours? I feel so very
thirsty, and I want to go and get some water. I'm
sure I don't know why I should be thirsty. Are
you, Aunt Mary? Ah! here it is. Don't disturb
yourself, aunty; I've found it. It was in my bag,

just where I'd put it myself. But all this trouble about Willis has made me so fidgety that I don't know where anything is. And now I don't know how to manage about the baby while I go after the water. He's sleeping soundly enough now; but if he should happen to get into one of his rolling moods, he might tumble out on to the floor. Never mind, aunty, I've thought of something. I'll just barricade him with these bags and shawls. Now, old fellow, roll as much as you like. If you should happen to hear him stir, aunty, won't you — Aunty! Oh, dear! she's asleep already; and what shall I do?" While *Mrs. Roberts* continues talking, various notes of protest, profane and otherwise, make themselves heard from different berths. "I know. I'll make a bold dash for the water, and be back in an instant, baby. Now, don't you move, you little rogue." She runs to the water-tank at the end of the car, and then back to her berth. "Now, baby, here's mamma again. Are you all right, mamma's own?" A shaggy head and bearded face are thrust from the curtains of the next berth.

The Stranger: "Look here, ma'am. I don't want to be disagreeable about this thing, and I hope you won't take any offence; but the fact is, I'm half dead for want of sleep, and if you'll only keep quiet now a little while, I'll promise not to speak above my breath if ever I find you on a sleeping-car after you've come straight through from San Francisco, day and night, and not been able to get more than about a quarter of your usual allowance of rest — I will indeed."

Mrs. Roberts: "I'm very sorry that I've disturbed you, and I'll try to be more quiet. I didn't suppose I was speaking so loud; but the cars keep up such a rattling that you never can tell how loud you *are* speaking. Did I understand you to say that you were from California?"

The Californian: "Yes, ma'am."

Mrs. Roberts: "San Francisco?"

The Californian: "Yes, ma'am."

Mrs. Roberts: "Thanks. It's a terribly long journey, isn't it? I know quite how to feel for you. I've a brother myself coming on. In fact, we expected him before this." She scans his face as sharply as the lamplight will allow, and continues, after a brief hesitation. "It's always such a silly question to ask a person, and I suppose San Francisco is a large place, with a great many people always coming and going, so that it would be only one chance in a thousand if you did."

The Californian, patiently: "Did what, ma'am?"

Mrs. Roberts: "Oh, I was just wondering if it was possible — but of course, it isn't, and it's very flat to ask — that you'd ever happened to meet my brother there. His name is Willis Campbell."

The Californian, with more interest: "Campbell? Campbell? Yes, I know a man of that name. But I disremember his first name. Little low fellow — pretty chunky?"

Mrs. Roberts: "I don't know. Do you mean short and stout?"

The Californian: "Yes, ma'am."

Mrs. Roberts: "I'm sure I can't tell. It's a great many years since he went out there, and I've never seen him in all that time. I thought if you *did* happen to know him — He's a lawyer."

The Californian: "It's quite likely I know him; and in the morning, ma'am" —

Mrs. Roberts: "Oh, excuse me. I'm very sorry to have kept you so long awake with my silly questions."

The Man in the Upper Berth: "Don't apologize, madam. I'm not a Californian myself, but I'm an orphan, and away from home, and I thank you, on behalf of all our fellow-passengers, for the mental refreshment that your conversation has afforded us. *I* could lie here, and listen to it all night; but there are invalids in some of these berths, and perhaps on their account it will be as well to defer everything till the morning, as our friend suggests. Allow me to wish you pleasant dreams, madam."

The Californian, while *Mrs. Roberts* shrinks back under the curtain of her berth in dismay, and stammers some inaudible excuse, slowly emerges full length from his berth: "Don't you mind me, ma'am; I've got everything but my boots and coat on. Now, then," standing beside the berth, and looking in upon the man in the upper tier. "You! Do you know that this is a lady you're talking to?"

The Upper Berth: "By your voice and your shaggy personal appearance I shouldn't have taken you for a lády — no, sir. But the light is very imperfect; you may be a bearded lady."

The Californian: "You never mind about my

looks. The question is, Do you want your head rapped up against the side of this car?"

The Upper Berth: "With all the frankness of your own Pacific Slope, no."

Mrs. Roberts, hastily re-appearing: "Oh, no, no, don't hurt him! He's not to blame. I was wrong to keep on talking. Oh, please don't hurt him!"

The Californian to *The Upper Berth:* "You hear? Well, now, don't you speak another word to that lady to-night. Just go on, ma'am, and free your mind on any little matter you like. *I* don't want any sleep. How long has your brother been in California?"

Mrs. Roberts: "Oh, don't let's talk about it now; I don't want to talk about it. I thought — I thought — Good-night. Oh, dear! I didn't suppose I was making so much trouble. I didn't mean to disturb anybody. I" — *Mrs. Roberts* gives way to the excess of her confusion and mortification in a little sob, and then hides her grief behind the curtains of her berth. *The Californian* slowly emerges again from his couch, and stands beside it, looking in upon the man in the berth above.

The Californian: "For half a cent I *would* rap your head up against that wall. Making the lady cry, and getting me so mad I can't sleep! Now see here, you just apologize. You beg that lady's pardon, or I'll have you out of there before you know yourself." Cries of "Good!" "That's right!" *and* "Make him show himself!" hail *Mrs. Roberts's* champion, and heads, more or less dishevelled, are thrust from every berth. *Mrs. Roberts* remains invisible and silent, and the loud and somewhat complicated respiration of her *Aunt* makes itself heard in the general hush of expectancy. A remark to the effect that "The old lady seems to enjoy her rest" achieves a facile applause. *The Californian* again addresses the culprit. "Come, now, what do you say? I'll give you just one-half a minute."

Mrs. Roberts from her shelter: "Oh, please, *please* don't make him say anything! It was very trying in me to keep him awake, and I know he didn't mean any offence. Oh, *do* let him be!"

The Californian: "You hear that? You stay quiet the rest of the time; and if that lady chooses to keep us all awake the whole night, don't *you* say a word, or I'll settle with you in the morning."

Loud and continued applause, amidst which *The Californian* turns from the man in the berth before him, and restores order by marching along the aisle of the car in his stocking feet. The heads vanish behind the curtains. As the laughter subsides, he returns to his berth, and after a stare up and down the tranquillized car, he is about to retire.

A Voice: "Oh, don't just bow! Speak!" A fresh burst of laughter greets this sally. *The Californian* erects himself again with an air of bated wrath, and then suddenly breaks into a helpless laugh.

The Californian: "Gentlemen, you're too many for *me.*" He gets into his berth, and after cries of "Good for California!" "You're all right, William Nye!" *and* "You're several ahead yet!" the occupants of the different berths gradually relapse into silence, and at last, as the car lunges onward through the darkness, nothing is heard but the rhythmical clank of the machinery, with now and then a burst of audible slumber from *Mrs. Roberts's Aunt Mary.*

II.

At Worcester, where the train has made the usual stop, *The Porter*, with his lantern on his arm, enters the car, preceding a gentleman somewhat anxiously smiling; his nervous speech contrasts painfully with the business-like impassiveness of *The Porter*, who refuses, with an air of incredulity, to enter into the confidences which the gentleman seems reluctant to bestow.

Mr. Edward Roberts: "This is the Governor Marcy, isn't it?"

The Porter: "Yes, sah."

Mr. Roberts: "Came on from Albany, and not from New York?"

The Porter: "Yes, sah, it did."

Mr. Roberts: "Ah! it must be all right. I" —

The Porter: "Was your wife expecting you to come on board here?"

Mr. Roberts: "Well, no, not exactly. She was expecting me to meet her at Boston. But I" —

struggling to give the situation dignity, but failing, and throwing himself, with self-convicted silliness, upon *The Porter's* mercy. "The fact is, I thought I would surprise her by joining her here."

The Porter, refusing to have any mercy: "Oh! How did you expect to find her?"

Mr. Roberts: "Well — well — I don't know. I didn't consider." He looks down the aisle in despair at the close-drawn curtains of the berths, and up at the dangling hats and bags and bonnets, and down at the chaos of boots of both sexes on the floor. "I don't know *how* I expected to find her." *Mr. Roberts's* countenance falls, and he visibly sinks so low in his own esteem and an imaginary public opinion that *The Porter* begins to have a little compassion.

The Porter: "Dey's so many ladies on board *I* couldn't find her."

Mr. Roberts: "Oh, no, no! of course not. I didn't expect that."

The Porter: "Don't like to go routing 'em all up, you know. I wouldn't be allowed to."

Mr. Roberts: "I don't ask it; that would be preposterous."

The Porter: "What sort of looking lady was she?"

Mr. Roberts: "Well, I don't know, really. Not very tall, rather slight, blue eyes. I — I don't know what you'd call her nose. And — stop! Oh, yes, she had a child with her, a little boy. Yes!"

The Porter, thoughtfully looking down the aisle: "Dey was three ladies had children. I didn't notice whether dey was boys or girls, or *what* dey was. Didn't have anybody with her?"

Mr. Roberts: "No, no. Only the child."

The Porter: "Well, I don't know what you are going to do, sah. It won't be a great while now till morning, you know. Here comes the conductor. Maybe he'll know what to do." *Mr. Roberts* makes some futile, inarticulate attempts to prevent *The Porter* from laying the case before *The Conductor*, and then stands guiltily smiling, overwhelmed with the hopeless absurdity of his position.

The Conductor, entering the car, and stopping before *The Porter*, and looking at *Mr. Roberts*. "Gentleman want a berth?"

The Porter, grinning: "Well, no, sah. He's lookin' for his wife."

The Conductor, with suspicion: "Is she aboard this car?"

Mr. Roberts, striving to propitiate *The Conductor* by a dastardly amiability: "Oh, yes, yes. There's no mistake about the car — the Governor Marcy. She telegraphed the name just before you left Albany, so that I could find her at Boston in the morning. Ah!"

The Conductor: "At Boston?" Sternly: "Then what are you trying to find her at Worcester in the middle of the night for?"

Mr. Roberts: "Why — I — that is" —

The Porter, taking compassion on *Mr. Roberts's* inability to continue: "Says he wanted to surprise her."

Mr. Roberts: "Ha — yes, exactly. A little caprice, you know."

The Conductor: "Well, that may all be so." *Mr. Roberts* continues to smile in agonized helplessness against *The Conductor's* injurious tone, which becomes more and more offensively patronizing. "But *I* can't do anything for you. Here are all these people asleep in their berths, and I can't go round waking them up because you want to surprise your wife."

Mr. Roberts: "No, no; of course not. I never thought" —

The Conductor: "My advice to *you* is to have a berth made up, and go to bed till we get to Boston, and surprise your wife by telling her what you tried to do."

Mr. Roberts, unable to resent the patronage of this suggestion: "Well, I don't know but I will."

The Conductor, going out: "The porter will make up the berth for you."

Mr. Roberts to *The Porter*, who is about to pull down the upper berth over a vacant seat: "Ah! Er — I — I don't think I'll trouble you to make it up; it's so near morning now. Just bring me a pillow, and I'll try to get a nap without lying down." He takes the vacant seat.

The Porter: "All right, sah." He goes to the end of the car, and returns with a pillow.

Mr. Roberts: "Ah — porter!"

The Porter: "Yes, sah."

Mr. Roberts: "Of course you didn't notice; but you don't think you *did* notice who was in that berth yonder?"

He indicates a certain berth.

The Porter: "Dat's a gen'leman in dat berth, I think, sah."

Mr. Roberts, astutely: "There's a bonnet hanging from the hook at the top. I'm not sure, but it looks like my wife's bonnet."

The Porter, evidently shaken by this reasoning, but recovering his firmness: "Yes, sah. But you can't depend upon de ladies to hang deir bonnets on de right hook. Jes' likely as not dat lady's took de hook at de foot of her berth instead o' de head. Sometimes dey takes both."

Mr. Roberts: "Ah!" After a pause. "Porter!"

The Porter: "Yes, sah."

Mr. Roberts: "You wouldn't feel justified in looking?"

The Porter: "I couldn't, sah; I couldn't, indeed."

Mr. Roberts, reaching his left hand towards *The Porter's,* and pressing a half-dollar into his instantly responsive palm: "But there's nothing to prevent *my* looking if I feel perfectly sure of the bonnet?"

The Porter: "N-no, sah."

Mr. Roberts: "All right."

The Porter retires to the end of the car, and

resumes the work of polishing the passengers' boots. After an interval of quiet, *Mr. Roberts* rises, and, looking about him with what he feels to be melodramatic stealth, approaches the suspected berth. He unloops the curtain with a trembling hand, and peers ineffectually in; he advances his head farther and farther into the darkened recess, and then suddenly dodges back again, with *The Californian* hanging to his neckcloth with one hand.

The Californian, savagely : "What do you want ? "

Mr. Roberts, struggling and breathless : "I — I — I want my wife."

The Californian : "Want your wife ! Have *I* got your wife ? "

Mr. Roberts : "No — ah — that is — ah, excuse me — I thought you *were* my wife."

The Californian, getting out of the berth, but at the same time keeping hold of *Mr. Roberts :* "Thought I was your *wife !* Do I look like your wife ? You can't play that on me, old man. Porter ! conductor ! "

Mr. Roberts, agonized : "Oh, I beseech you, my dear sir, don't — don't ! I can explain it —

I can indeed. I know it has an ugly look ; but if you will allow me two words — only two words " —

Mrs. Roberts, suddenly parting the curtain of her berth, and springing out into the aisle, with her hair wildly dishevelled : " Edward ! "

Mr. Roberts : " Oh, Agnes, explain to this gentleman ! " Imploringly : " Don't you know me ? "

A Voice : " Make him show you the strawberry mark on his left arm."

Mrs. Roberts : " Edward ! Edward ! " *The Californian* mechanically loses his grip, and they fly into each other's embrace. " *Where* did you come from ? "

A Voice : " Centre door, left hand, one back."

The Conductor, returning with his lantern : " Hallo ! What's the matter here ? "

A Voice : " Train robbers ! Throw up your hands ! Tell the express-messenger to bring his safe." The passengers emerge from their berths in various *deshabille* and bewilderment.

The Conductor to *Mr. Roberts :* " Have *you* been making all this row, waking up my passengers ? "

The Californian : "No, sir, he hasn't. *I've* been making this row. This gentleman was peaceably looking for his wife, and I misunderstood him. You want to say anything to *me?* "

The Conductor, silently taking *The Californian's* measure with his eye, as he stands six feet in his stockings : "If I did I'd get the biggest brakeman I could find to do it for me. *I've* got nothing to say except that I think you'd better all go back to bed again." He goes out, and the passengers disappear one by one, leaving the *Robertses* and *The Californian* alone.

The Californian, to *Mr. Roberts :* "Stranger, I'm sorry I got you into this scrape."

Mr. Roberts : "Oh, don't speak of it, my dear sir. I'm sure we owe you all sorts of apologies, which I shall be most happy to offer you at my house in Boston, with every needful explanation." He takes out his card, and gives it to *The Californian,* who looks at it, and then looks at *Mr. Roberts* curiously. "There's my address. and I'm sure we shall both be glad to have you call."

Mrs. Roberts : "Oh, yes, indeed." *The Californian* parts the curtains of his berth to re-enter it. "Good-night, sir, and I assure you *we* shall do nothing more to disturb you — shall we, Edward ?"

Mr. Roberts : "No.   And now, dear, I think you'd better go back to your berth."

Mrs. Roberts : "I couldn't sleep, and I shall not go back.   Is this your place ?   I will just rest my head on your shoulder ; and we must both be perfectly quiet.   You've no idea what a nuisance I have been making of myself.   The whole car was perfectly furious at me one time, I kept talking so loud.   I don't know how I came to do it, but I suppose it was thinking about you and Willis meeting without knowing each other made me nervous, and I couldn't be still.   I woke everybody up with my talking, and some of them were quite outrageous in their remarks ; but I didn't blame them the least bit, for I should have been just as bad.   That California gentleman was perfectly splendid, though.   I can tell you *he* made them stop.   We struck up quite a friendship.   I told him I had a brother coming on from California, and he's going to try to think whether he knows Willis."   Groans and inarticulate protests make themselves heard from different berths.   "I de-

clare, I've got to talking again! There, now, I
shall stop, and they won't hear another squeak
from me the rest of the night." She lifts her head
from her husband's shoulder. "I wonder if baby
will roll out. He *does* kick so! And I just sprang
up and left him when I heard your voice, without
putting anything to keep him in. I *must* go and
have a look at him, or I never can settle down.
No, no, don't you go, Edward; you'll be prying
into all the wrong berths in the car, you poor
thing! You stay here, and I'll be back in half a
second. I wonder which is my berth. Ah! that's
it; I know the one now." She makes a sudden
dash at a berth, and pulling open the curtains is
confronted by the bearded visage of *The Californian.* "Ah! Ow! ow! Edward! Ah! I — I
beg your pardon, sir; excuse me; I didn't know it
was you. I came for my baby."

The Californian, solemnly: "I haven't got any
baby, ma'am."

Mrs. Roberts: "No — no — I thought *you* were
my baby."

The Californian: "Perhaps I am, ma'am; I've
lost so much sleep I could cry, anyway. Do I
look like your baby?"

Mrs. Roberts : "No, no, you don't." In distress that overcomes her mortification. "Oh, where *is* my baby ? I left him all uncovered, and he'll take his death of cold, even if he doesn't roll out. Oh, Edward, Edward, help me to find baby ! "

Mr. Roberts, bustling aimlessly about: "Yes, yes ; certainly, my dear. But don't be alarmed ; we shall find him."

The Californian, getting out in his stocking feet : "We shall find him, ma'am, if we have to search every berth in this car. Don't you take on. That baby's going to be found if he's aboard the train, now, you bet ! " He looks about and then tears open the curtains of a berth at random. "That your baby, ma'am ? "

Mrs. Roberts, flying upon the infant thus exposed. "Oh, *baby*, baby, baby ! I thought I had lost you. Um ! um ! um ! " She clasps him in her arms, and covers his face and neck with kisses.

The Californian, as he gets back into his berth, *sotto voce :* "I wish I *had* been her baby."

Mrs. Roberts, returning with her husband to his seat, and bringing the baby with her:

"There! Did you ever *see* such a sleeper, Edward?" In her ecstasy she abandons all control of her voice, and joyfully exclaims: "He has slept all through this excitement, without a wink."

A solemn *Voice* from one of the berths: "I envy him." A laugh follows, in which all the passengers join.

Mrs. Roberts, in a hoarse whisper, breaking a little with laughter: "Oh, my goodness! there I went again. But how funny! I assure you, Edward, that if their remarks had not been about me, I could have really quite enjoyed some of them. I wish there had been somebody here to take them down. And I hope I shall see some of the speakers in the morning before — Edward, I've got an idea!"

Mr. Roberts, endeavoring to teach his wife by example to lower her voice, which has risen again: "What — what is it, my dear?"

Mrs. Roberts: "Why, don't you see? How perfectly ridiculous it was of me not to think of it before! though I did think of it once, and hadn't the courage to insist upon it. But of course it is; and it accounts for his being so polite and kind to me through all, and it's the only thing that can. Yes, yes, it *must* be."

Mr. Roberts, mystified : " What ? "

Mrs. Roberts : " Willis."

Mr. Roberts : " Who ? "

Mrs. Roberts : " This Californian."

Mr. Roberts : " Oh ! "

Mrs. Roberts : " No *stranger* could have been so patient, and — and — attentive ; and I know that he recognized me from the first, and he's just kept it up for a joke, so as to surprise us, and have a good laugh at us when we get to Boston. Of *course* it's Willis."

Mr. Roberts, doubtfully : " Do you think so, my dear ? "

Mrs. Roberts : " I *know* it. Didn't you notice how he looked at your card ? And I want you to go at once and speak to him, and turn the tables on him."

Mr. Roberts : " I — I'd rather *not*, my dear."

Mrs. Roberts : " Why, Edward, what can you mean ? "

Mr. Roberts : " He's very violent. Suppose it *shouldn't* be Willis ? "

Mrs. Roberts : " Nonsense ! It *is* Willis. Come,

let's both go and just tax him with it. He can't deny it, after all he's done for me." She pulls her reluctant husband toward *The Californian's* berth, and they each draw a curtain. "Willis!"

The Californian, with plaintive endurance: "Well, ma'am?"

Mrs. Roberts, triumphantly: "There! I knew it was you all along. How could you play such a joke on me?"

The Californian: "I didn't know there'd been any joke; but I suppose there must have been, if you say so. Who am I now, ma'am — you husband, or your baby, or your husband's wife, or" —

Mrs. Roberts: "How funny you are! You *know* you're Willis Campbell, my only brother. Now *don't* try to keep it up any longer, Willis."

Voices, from various berths: "Give us a rest, Willis!" "Joke's too thin, Willis!' "You're played out, Willis!" "Own up, old fellow — own up!"

The Californian, issuing from his berth, and walking up and down the aisle, as before, till quiet is restored: "I haven't got any sister, and my name ain't Willis, and it ain't Campbell. I'm very sorry, because I'd like to oblige you any way I could."

Mrs. Roberts, in deep mortification : " It's I who ought to apologize, and I do most humbly. I don't know what to say; but when I got to thinking about it, and how kind you had been to me, and how sweet you had been under all my — interruptions, I felt perfectly sure that you couldn't be a mere stranger, and then the idea struck me that you must be my brother in disguise; and I was so certain of it that I couldn't help just letting you know that we'd found you out, and " —

Mr. Roberts, offering a belated and feeble moral support : " Yes."

Mrs. Roberts, promptly turning upon him : " And *you* ought to have kept me from making such a simpleton of myself, Edward."

The Californian, soothingly : " Well, ma'am, that ain't always so easy. A man may mean well, and yet not be able to carry out his intentions. But it's all right. And I reckon we'd better try to quiet down again, and get what rest we can."

Mrs. Roberts : " Why, yes, certainly ; and I will try — oh, I will *try* not to disturb you again. And if there's anything we can do in reparation after we reach Boston, we shall be *so* glad to do it!"

They bow themselves away, and return to their seat, while *The Californian* re-enters his berth.

III.

THE train stops at Framingham, and *The Porter* comes in with a passenger, whom he shows to the seat opposite *Mr. and Mrs. Roberts*.

The Porter: "You can sit here, sah. We'll be in, in about half an hour now. Hang up your bag for you, sah ? "

The Passenger: "No, leave it on the seat here."

The Porter goes out, and the *Robertses* maintain a dejected silence. The bottom of the bag, thrown carelessly on the seat, is toward the *Robertses*, who regard it listlessly.

Mrs. Roberts, suddenly clutching her husband's arm, and hissing in his ear: "See ! " She points to the white lettering on the bag, where the name "Willis Campbell, San Francisco," is distinctly legible. "But it can't be ; it must be some other Campbell. I can't risk it."

Mr. Roberts: "But there's the name. It would

be very strange if there were two people from San Francisco of exactly the same name. *I* will speak."

Mrs. Roberts, as wildly as one can in whisper: " No, no, I can't let you. We've made ourselves the laughing-stock of the whole car already with our mistakes, and I can't go on. I would rather perish than ask him. You don't suppose it *could* be ? No, it couldn't. There may be twenty Willis Campbells in San Francisco, and there probably are. Do you think he looks like me ? He has a straight nose; but you can't tell anything about the lower part of his face, the beard covers it so; and I can't make out the color of his eyes by this light. But of course, it's all nonsense. Still, if it *should* be ! It would be very stupid of us to ride all the way from Framingham to Boston with that name staring one in the eyes. I *wish* he would turn it away. If it really turned out to *be* Willis, he would think we were awfully stiff and cold. But I can't help it; I *can't* go attacking every stranger I see, and accusing him of being my brother. No, no, I can't, and I *won't*, and that's all about it." She leans forward, and addresses the stranger with sudden sweetness. "Excuse me, sir, but I *am* very much interested by the name on your bag. Not that I think you are even acquainted with him, and there are probably a great many of them there; but your coming from the same city, and all, *does* seem a little queer, and I hope you won't think me intrusive in speaking to you, because if you *should* happen, by the thousandth of 'a chance, to be the right one, I should be *so* happy !"

Campbell : "The right what, madam ? "

Mrs. Roberts : "The right Willis Campbell."

Campbell : "I hope I'm not the wrong one; though after a week's pull on the railroad it's pretty hard for a man to tell which Willis Campbell he is. May I ask if your Willis Campbell had friends in Boston ?"

Mrs. Roberts, eagerly : "He had a sister and a brother-in-law and a nephew."

Campbell : "Name of Roberts ?"

Mrs. Roberts : "Every one."

Campbell : "Then you're " —

Mrs. Roberts, ecstatically : "Agnes."

Campbell : "And he's " —

Mrs. Roberts : "Mr. Roberts !"

Campbell : "And the baby's" —

Mrs. Roberts : " Asleep ! "

Campbell : " Then I *am* the right one."

Mrs. Roberts : " Oh, Willis ! Willis ! Willis ! To think of our meeting in this way ! " She kisses and embraces him, while *Mr. Roberts* shakes one of his hands which he finds disengaged. " *How* in the world did it happen ? "

Campbell : "Oh, I found myself a little ahead of time, and I stopped off with an old friend of mine at Framingham ; I didn't want to disappoint you when you came to meet this train, or get you up last night at midnight."

Mrs. Roberts : " And I was in Albany, and I've been moving heaven and earth to get home before you arrived ; and Edward came aboard at Worcester to surprise me, and — Oh, you've never seen the baby ! I'll run right and get him this instant, just as he is, and bring him. Edward, you be explaining to Willis — Oh, my goodness ! " looking wildly about. "I don't remember the berth, and I shall be sure to wake up that poor California gentleman again. *What* shall I do ? "

Campbell : "What California gentleman ? "

Mrs. Roberts : " Oh, somebody we've been stirring up the whole blessed night. First I took him for baby, and then Edward took him for me, and then I took him for baby again, and then we both took him for you."

Campbell : "Did he look like any of us ? "

Mrs. Roberts : "Like *us?* He's eight feet tall, if he's an inch, in his stockings — and he's always in them — and he has a long black beard and mustaches, and he's very lanky, and stoops over a good deal; but he's just as lovely as he can be, and live, and he's been as kind and patient as twenty Jobs."

Campbell : "Speaks in a sort of soft, slow grind ? "

Mrs. Roberts : " Yes."

Campbell : " Gentle and deferential to ladies ? "

Mrs. Roberts : "As pie."

Campbell : "It's Tom Goodall. I'll have him out of there in half a second. I want you to take him home with you, Agnes. He's the best fellow in the world. *Which* is his berth ? "

Mrs. Roberts : "Don't ask me, Willis. But if you'd go for baby, you'll be sure to find *him.*"

Mr. Roberts, timidly indicating a berth: "I think that's the one."

Campbell, plunging at it, and pulling the cur-tains open : " You, old Tom Goodall ! "

The Californian, appearing : " I ain't any Tom Goodall. My name's Abram Sawyer."

Campbell, falling back : " Well, sir, you're right. I'm awfully sorry to disturb you; but, from my sister's description here, I felt certain you must be my old friend Tom Goodall."

The Californian : " I ain't surprised at it. I'm only surprised I *ain't* Tom Goodall. I've been a baby twice, and I've been a man's wife once, and once I've been a long-lost brother."

Campbell, laughing : " Oh, they've found *him.* *I'm* the long-lost brother."

The Californian, sleepily : " Has she found the other one ? "

Campbell : " Yes; all right, I believe."

The Californian : " Has *he* found what *he* wanted ? "

Campbell : " Yes; we're all together here." *The Californian* makes a movement to get into bed again. " Oh, don't! You'd better make a night of it now. It's almost morning anyway. We want you to go home with us, and Mrs. Roberts will give you a bed at her house, and let you sleep a week."

The Californian : " Well, I reckon you're right,

stranger. I seem to be in the hands of Providence to-night, anyhow." He pulls on his boots and coat, and takes his seat beside *Campbell*. "I reckon there ain't any use in fighting against Providence."

Mrs. Roberts, briskly, as if she had often tried it and failed: "Oh, not the least in the world. I'm sure it was all intended; and if you had turned out to be Willis at last, I should be *certain* of it. What surprises me is that you shouldn't turn out to be anybody, after all."

The Californian: "Yes, it is kind of curious. But I couldn't help it. I did my best."

Mrs. Roberts: "Oh, don't speak of it. *We* are the ones who ought to apologize. But if you only had been somebody, it would have been such a good joke! We could always have had such a laugh over it, don't you see?"

The Californian: "Yes, ma'am, it would have been funny. But I hope you've enjoyed it as it is."

Mrs. Roberts: "Oh, very much, thanks to you. Only I can't seem to get reconciled to your not being anybody, after all. You *must* at least be some one we've heard about, don't you think?

It's so strange that you and Willis never even met. Don't you think you have some acquaintances in common ? "

Campbell : "Look here, Agnes, do you always shout at the top of your voice in this way when you converse in a sleeping-car ? "

Mrs. Roberts : "Was I talking loud again ? Well, you can't help it, if you want to make people hear you."

Campbell : "But there must be a lot of them who don't want to hear you. I wonder that the passengers who are not blood-relations don't throw things at you — boots and hand-bags and language."

Mrs. Roberts : "Why, that's what they've *been* doing — language at least — and I'm only surprised they're not doing it now."

The Californian, rising : "They'd better not, ma'am." He patrols the car from end to end, and quells some rising murmurs, halting at the rebellious berths as he passes.

Mrs. Roberts, enraptured by his championship : "Oh, he *must* be some connection." She glances through the window. "I do believe that was Newton, or Newtonville, or West Newton, or

Newton Centre. I must run and wake up baby, and get him dressed. I sha'n't want to wait an instant after we get in. Why, we're slowing up! Why, I do believe we're there! Edward, we're there! Only fancy being there already!"

Mr. Roberts: "Yes, my dear. Only we're not quite there yet. Hadn't we better call your Aunt Mary?"

Mrs. Roberts: "I'd forgotten her."

Campbell: "Is Aunt Mary with you?"

Mrs. Roberts: "To be sure she is. Didn't I tell you? She came on expressly to meet you."

Campbell, starting up impetuously: "Which berth is she in?"

Mrs. Roberts: "Right over baby."

Campbell: "And which berth is baby in?"

Mrs. Roberts, distractedly: "Why, that's just what I can't *tell.* It was bad enough when they were all filled up; but now, since the people have begun to come out of them, and some of them are made into seats, I *can't* tell."

The Californian: "I'll look for you, ma'am. I should like to wake up all the wrong passengers on this car. I'd take a pleasure in it. If you

could make sure of any berth that *ain't* the one,
I'd begin on that."

Mrs. Roberts: "I can't even be sure of the
wrong one. No, no; you mustn't " — *The Californian* moves away, and pauses in front of one
of the berths, looking back inquiringly at *Mrs.
Roberts.* "Oh, don't ask *me! I* can't tell." To
Campbell: "Isn't he amusing? So like all those
Californians that one reads of — so chivalrous and
so humorous !"

Aunt Mary, thrusting her head from the curtains
of the berth before which *The California* is
standing: "Go along with you! What do you
want ? "

The Californian: "Aunt Mary."

Aunt Mary: "Go away. Aunt Mary, indeed!"

Mrs. Roberts, turning toward her, followed by
Campbell and *Mr. Roberts:* "Why, Aunt Mary,
it *is* you ! And here's Willis, and here's Edward."

Aunt Mary: "Nonsense! How did they get
aboard ? "

Mrs. Roberts: "Edward came on at Worcester,
and Willis at Framingham, to surprise me."

Aunt Mary: "And a very silly performance.
Let them wait till I'm dressed, and then I'll talk

to them. Send for the porter." She withdraws her head behind the curtain, and then thrusts it out again. " And who, pray, may *this* be ? " She indicates *The Californian.*

Mrs. Roberts : "Oh, a friend of ours from California, who's been so kind to us all night, and who's going home with us."

Aunt Mary : "Another ridiculous surprise, I suppose. But he shall not surprise *me.* Young man, isn't your name Sawyer ? "

The Californian : "Yes, ma'am."

Aunt Mary : " Abram ? "

The Californian : "Abram Sawyer. You're right there, ma'am." .

Mrs. Roberts : "Oh ! oh ! I knew it ! I knew that he must be somebody belonging to us. Oh, thank you, aunty, for thinking " —

Aunt Mary : "Don't be absurd, Agnes. Then you're my " —

A Voice from one of the berths : "Long-lost stepson. Found ! found at last ! "

The Californian looks vainly round in an endeavor to identify the speaker, and then turns again to *Aunt Mary.*

Aunt Mary : "Weren't your parents from Bath ? "

The Californian, eagerly : "Both of 'em, ma'am — both of 'em."

The Voice : " O my prophetic soul, my uncle ! "

Aunt Mary : " Then you're my old friend Kate Harris's daughter ? "

The Californian : " I might be her *son,* ma'am; but *my* mother's name was Susan Wakeman."

Aunt Mary, in sharp disgust : " Call the porter, please." She withdraws her head and pulls her curtains together; the rest look blankly at one another.

Campbell : " Another failure, and just when we thought we were sure of you. I don't know what we shall do about you, Mr. Sawyer."

The Voice : " Adopt him."

Campbell : " That's a good idea. We will adopt you. You shall be our adoptive " —

The Voice : " Baby boy."

Another Voice : " Wife."

A Third Voice : " Brother."

A Fourth Voice : " Early friend."

A Fifth Voice : " Kate Harris's daughter."

Campbell, laying his hand on *The Californian's* shoulder, and breaking into a laugh : " Don't mind them. They don't mean anything. It's just their way. You come home with my sister, and spend Christmas, and let us devote the rest of our lives to making your declining years happy."

Voices : " Good for you, Willis ! " " We'll all come ! " " No ceremony ! " " Small and early ! "

Campbell, looking round : " We appear to have fallen in with a party of dry-goods drummers. It makes a gentleman feel like an intruder." The train stops ; he looks out of the window. " We've arrived. Come, Agnes ; come, Roberts ; come, Mr. Sawyer — let's be going." They gather up their several wraps and bags, and move with great dignity toward the door.

Aunt Mary, putting out her head : " Agnes ! If you must forget your aunt, at least remember your child."

Mrs. Roberts, running back in an agony of remorse : " Oh, *baby,* did I forget you ? "

Campbell : " Oh, *aunty,* did she forget you ? " He runs back, and extends his arms to his aunt. " Let me help you down, Aunt Mary."

Aunt Mary : "Nonsense, Willis. Send the porter."

Campbell, turning round and confronting *The Porter :* "He was here upon instinct. Shall he fetch a step-ladder ? "

Aunt Mary : "He will know what to do. Go away, Willis; go away with that child, Agnes. If I should happen to fall on you " — They retreat; the curtain drops and her voice is heard behind it addressing *The Porter :* " Give me your hand; now your back; now your knee. So! And very well done, thanks."

THE REGISTER.

FARCE.

THE REGISTER.

Farce.

I.

SCENE : In an upper chamber of a boarding-house in Melanchthon Place, Boston, a mature, plain young lady, with every appearance of establishing herself in the room for the first time, moves about, bestowing little touches of decoration here and there, and talking with another young lady, whose voice comes through the open doorway of an inner room.

Miss Ethel Reed, from within : "What in the world are you doing, Nettie ? "

Miss Henrietta Spaulding : "Oh, sticking up a household god or two. What are you doing ? "

Miss Reed : "Despairing."

Miss Spaulding : "Still ? "

Miss Reed, tragically : "*Still !* How soon did you expect me to stop ? I am here on the sofa, where I flung myself two hours ago, and I don't think I shall ever get up.   There is no reason *why* I ever should."

Miss Spaulding, suggestively : " Dinner."

Miss Reed : " Oh, dinner !   Dinner, to a broken heart ! "

Miss Spaulding : " I don't believe your heart is broken."

Miss Reed : " But I tell you it is !   I ought to know when my own heart is broken, I should hope.   What makes you think it isn't ? "

Miss Spaulding : " Oh, it's happened so often ! "

Miss Reed : " But this is a real case.   You ought to feel my forehead.   It's as *hot !* "

Miss Spaulding : " You ought to get up and help me put this room to rights, and then you would feel better."

Miss Reed : " No ; I should feel worse.   The idea of household gods makes me sick.   Sylvan deities are what *I* want; the great god Pan among the cat-tails and arrow-heads in the ' ma'sh ' at Ponk-wasset; the dryads of the birch woods — there are no oaks; the nymphs that haunt the heights and hollows of the dear old mountain; the " —

Miss Spaulding : " Wha-a-at ?   I can't hear a word you say."

Miss Reed : "That's because you keep fussing about so. Why don't you be quiet, if you want to hear?" She lifts her voice to its highest pitch, with a pause for distinctness between the words : "I'm heart-broken for — Ponkwasset. The dryads — of the — birch woods. The nymphs — and the great — god — Pan — in the reeds — by the river. And all — that — sort of — thing!"

Miss Spaulding : "You know very well you're not."

Miss Reed : "I'm not? What's the reason I'm not? Then, what am I heart-broken for?"

Miss Spaulding : "You're not heart-broken at all. You know very well that he'll call before we've been here twenty-four hours."

Miss Reed : "Who?"

Miss Spaulding : "The great god Pan."

Miss Reed : "Oh, how cruel you are, to mock me so! Come in here, and sympathize a little! Do, Nettie."

Miss Spaulding : "No; you come out here and utilize a little. I'm acting for your best good, as they say at Ponkwasset."

Miss Reed : "When they want to be disagreeable!"

Miss Spaulding: "If this room isn't in order by the time he calls, you'll be everlastingly disgraced."

Miss Reed: "I'm that now. I can't be more so — there's that comfort. What makes you think he'll call?"

Miss Spaulding: "Because he's a gentleman, and will want to apologize. He behaved very rudely to you."

Miss Reed: "No, Nettie; *I* behaved rudely to *him.* Yes! Besides, if he behaved rudely, he was no gentleman. It's a contradiction in terms, don't you see? But I'll tell you what I'm going to do if he comes. I'm going to show a proper spirit for once in my life. I'm going to refuse to see him. *You've* got to see him."

Miss Spaulding: "Nonsense!"

Miss Reed: "Why nonsense? Oh, why? Expound!"

Miss Spaulding: "Because he wasn't rude to me, and he doesn't want to see me. Because I'm plain, and you're pretty."

Miss Reed: "I'm *not!* You know it perfectly well. I'm hideous."

Miss Spaulding: "Because I'm poor, and you're a person of independent property."

Miss Reed: "*Dependent* property, I should call it: just enough to be useless on! But that's insulting to. *him.* How can you say it's because I have a little money?"

Miss Spaulding: "Well, then, I won't. I take it back. I'll say it's because you're young, and I'm old."

Miss Reed: "You're *not* old. You're as young as anybody, Nettie Spaulding. And you know I'm not young; I'm twenty-seven, if I'm a day. I'm just dropping into the grave. But I can't argue with you, miles off so, any longer." *Miss Reed* appears at the open door, dragging languidly after her the shawl which she had evidently drawn round her on the sofa; her fair hair is a little disordered, and she presses it into shape with one hand as she comes forward; a lovely flush vies with a heavenly pallor in her cheeks; she looks a little pensive in the arching eyebrows, and a little humorous about the dimpled mouth. "Now I can prove that you are entirely wrong. Where were you? — This room *is* rather an improvement over the one we had last winter. There is more of a view" — she goes to the window — "of the houses across the Place; and I always think the

swell front gives a pretty shape to a room. I'm
sorry they've stopped building them. Your piano
goes very nicely into that little alcove. Yes,
we're quite palatial. And, on the whole, I'm
glad there's no fireplace. It's a pleasure at times;
but for the most part it's a vanity and a vexation,
getting dust and ashes over everything. Yes;
after all, give me the good old-fashioned, clean,
convenient register! Ugh! My feet are like ice."
She pulls an easy-chair up to the register in the
corner of the room, and pushes open its valves
with the toe of her slipper. As she settles herself luxuriously in the chair, and poises her feet
daintily over the register: "Ah, this is something like! Henrietta Spaulding, ma'am! Did I
ever tell you that you were the best friend I have
in the world?"

Miss Spaulding, who continues her work of
arranging the room: "Often."

Miss Reed: "Did you ever believe it?"

Miss Spaulding: "Never."

Miss Reed: "Why?"

Miss Spaulding, thoughtfully regarding a vase
which she holds in her hand, after several times
shifting it from a bracket to the corner of her

piano and back: "I wish I could tell where you *do* look best!"

Miss Reed, leaning forward wistfully, with her hands clasped and resting on her knees: "I wish you would tell me *why* you don't believe you're the best friend I have in the world."

Miss Spaulding, finally placing the vase on the bracket: "Because you've said so too often."

Miss Reed: "Oh, that's no reason! I can prove to you that you are. Who else but you would have taken in a homeless and friendless creature like me, and let her stay bothering round in demoralizing idleness, while you were seriously teaching the young idea how to drub the piano?"

Miss Spaulding: "Anybody who wanted a room-mate as much as I did, and could have found one willing to pay more than her share of the lodging."

Miss Reed, thoughtfully: "Do you think so, Henrietta?"

Miss Spaulding: "I know so."

Miss Reed: "And you're not afraid that you wrong yourself?"

Miss Spaulding: "Not the least."

Miss Reed: "Well, be it so — as they say in novels. I will not contradict you; I will not say you are my *best* friend; I will merely say that you are my *only* friend. Come here, Henrietta. Draw up your chair, and put your little hand in mine."

Miss Spaulding, with severe distrust: "What do you want, Ethel Reed?"

Miss Reed: "I want — I want — to talk it over with you."

Miss Spaulding, recoiling: "I knew it! Well, now, we've talked it over enough; we've talked it over till there's nothing left of it."

Miss Reed: "Oh, there's everything left! It remains in all its original enormity. Perhaps we shall get some new light upon it." She extends a pleading hand towards *Miss Spaulding.* "Come, Henrietta, my only friend, shake! — as the 'good Indians' say. Let your Ethel pour her hackneyed sorrows into your bosom. Such an uncomfortable image, it always seems, doesn't it, pouring sorrows into bosoms! Come!"

Miss Spaulding, decidedly: "No, I won't! And you needn't try wheedling any longer. I won't sympathize with you on that basis at all."

Miss Reed: "What shall I try, then, if you won't let me try · wheedling ? "

Miss Spaulding, going to the piano and opening it: " Try courage ; try self-respect."

Miss Reed : "Oh, dear ! when I haven't a morsel of either. Are you going to practise, you cruel maid ? "

Miss Spaulding : " Of course I am. It's half-past four, and if I don't do it now I sha'n't be prepared to-morrow for Miss Robins: she takes this piece."

Miss Reed : "Well, well, perhaps it's all for the best. If music be the food of — umph-ump ! — you know what !— play on." They both laugh, and *Miss Spaulding* pushes back a little from the piano, and wheels toward her friend, letting one hand rest slightly on the keys.

Miss Spaulding : "Ethel Reed, you're the most ridiculous girl in the world."

Miss Reed : " Correct ! "

Miss Spaulding : " And I don't believe you ever were in love, or ever will be."

Miss Reed : " Ah, there you wrong me, Henrietta ! I have been, and I shall be — lots of times."

Miss Spaulding: "Well, what do you want to say now? You must hurry, for I can't lose any more time."

Miss Reed: "I will free my mind with neatness and despatch. I simply wish to go over the whole affair, from Alfred to Omaha; and you've got to let me talk as much slang and nonsense as I want. And then I'll skip all the details I can. Will you?"

Miss Spaulding, with impatient patience: "Oh, I suppose so!"

Miss Reed: "That's very sweet of you, though you don't look it. Now, where was I? Oh, yes; do you think it was forth-putting at all, to ask him if he would give me the lessons?"

Miss Spaulding: "It depends upon why you asked him."

Miss Reed: "I asked him from — from — Let me see; I asked him because — from — Yes, I say it boldly; I asked him from an enthusiasm for art, and a sincere wish to learn the use of oil, as he called it. Yes!"

Miss Spaulding: "Are you sure?"

Miss Reed: "Sure? Well, we will say that I am, for the sake of argument. And, having secured this basis, the question is whether I wasn't bound to offer him pay at the end, and whether he wasn't wrong to take my doing so in dudgeon."

Miss Spaulding: "Yes, I think he was wrong. And the terms of his refusal were very ungentlemanly. He ought to apologize most amply and humbly." At a certain expression in *Miss Reed's* face, she adds, with severity: "Unless you're keeping back the main point. You usually do. Are you?"

Miss Reed: "No, no. I've told you everything —everything!"

Miss Spaulding: "Then I say, as I said from the beginning, that he behaved very badly. It was very awkward and very painful, but you've really nothing to blame yourself for."

Miss Reed, ruefully: "No-o-o!"

Miss Spaulding: "What do you mean by that sort of 'No'?"

Miss Reed: "Nothing."

Miss Spaulding, sternly: "Yes, you do, Ethel."

Miss Reed: "I don't, really. What makes you think I do?"

Miss Spaulding: "It sounded very dishonest."

Miss Reed: "Did it? I didn't mean it to."
Her friend breaks down with a laugh, while *Miss
Reed* preserves a demure countenance.

Miss Spaulding: "What *are* you keeping
back?"

Miss Reed: "Nothing at all—less than nothing! I never thought it was worth mentioning."

Miss Spaulding: "Are you telling me the
truth?"

Miss Reed: "I'm telling you the truth and
something more. You can't ask better than that,
can you?"

Miss Spaulding, turning to her music again:
"Certainly not."

Miss Reed: in a pathetic wail: "O Henrietta!
do you abandon me thus? Well, I will tell you,
heartless girl! I've only kept it back till now
because it was so extremely mortifying to my
pride as an artist—as a student of oil. Will
you hear me?"

Miss Spaulding, beginning to play: "No."

Miss Reed, with burlesque wildness: "You
shall!" *Miss Spaulding* involuntarily desists.
"There was a moment—a fatal moment—when
he said he thought he ought to tell me that if

I found oil amusing I could go on; but that he didn't believe I should ever learn to use it, and he couldn't let me take lessons from him with the expectation that I should. There!"

' *Miss Spaulding*, with awful reproach : "And you call that less than nothing ? I've almost a mind never to speak to you again, Ethel. How *could* you deceive me so ? "

Miss Reed : "Was it really deceiving ? *I* shouldn't call it so. And I needed your sympathy so much, and I knew I shouldn't get it unless you thought I was altogether in the right."

Miss Spaulding : "You are altogether in the *wrong !* And it's *you* that ought to apologize to *him* — on your bended knees. How *could* you offer him money after that ? I wonder at you, Ethel !"

Miss Reed : "Why — don't you see, Nettie ? — I did keep on taking the lessons of him. I did find oil amusing — or the oilist — and I kept on. Of course I had to, off there in a farmhouse full of lady boarders, and he the only gentleman short of Crawford's. Strike, but hear me, Henrietta Spaulding ! What was I to do about the half-dozen lessons I had taken before he told me I

should never learn to use oil ? Was I to offer
to pay him for these, and not for the rest; or
was I to treat the whole series as gratuitous ?
I used to lie awake thinking about it. I've got
some little tact, but I couldn't find any way out
of the trouble. It was a box — yes, a box of
the deepest dye ! And the whole affair having
got to be — something else, don't you know ? —
made it all the worse. And if he'd only — only —
But he didn't. Not a syllable, not a breath !
And there I was. I *had* to offer him the money.
And it's almost killed me — the way he took my
offering it, and now the way you take it ! And
it's all of a piece." *Miss Reed* suddenly snatches
her handkerchief from her pocket, and buries her
face in it. — " Oh, dear — oh, dear ! Oh ! — hu, hu,
hu ! "

Miss Spaulding, relenting : " It was awkward."

Miss Reed : " Awkward ! You seem to think
that because I carry things off lightly I have no
feeling."

Miss Spaulding : " You know I don't think that,
Ethel."

Miss Reed, pursuing her advantage : "I don't
know it from you, Nettie. I've tried and *tried* to

pass it off as a joke, and to treat it as something funny; but I can tell you it's no joke at all."

Miss Spaulding, sympathetically : " I see, dear."

Miss Reed : "It's not that I care for him " —

Miss Spaulding : "Why, of course."

Miss Reed : "For I don't in the least. He is horrid every way: blunt, and rude, and horrid. I never cared for him. But I care for myself! He has put me in the position of having done an unkind thing — an unladylike thing — when I was only doing what I had to do. Why need he have taken it the way he did ? Why couldn't he have said politely that he couldn't accept the money because he hadn't earned it ? Even *that* would have been mortifying enough. But he must go and be so violent, and rush off, and — Oh, I never could have treated anybody so ! "

Miss Spaulding : " Not unless you were very fond of them."

Miss Reed : " What ? "

Miss Spaulding : "Not unless you were very fond of them."

Miss Reed, putting away her handkerchief: " Oh, nonsense, Nettie ! He never cared anything for me, or he couldn't have acted so. But no matter for that. He has fixed everything so that it can never be got straight — never in the world. It will just have to remain a hideous mass of — of — *I* don't know what; and I have simply got to go on withering with despair at the point where I left off. But I don't care! That's one comfort."

Miss Spaulding: "I don't believe he'll let you wither long, Ethel."

Miss Reed: "He's let me wither for twenty-four hours already! But it's nothing to me, now, *how* long he lets me wither. I'm perfectly satisfied to have the affair remain as it is. I am in the right, and if he comes I shall refuse to see him."

Miss Spaulding: "Oh, no, you won't, Ethel!"

Miss Reed: "Yes, I shall. I shall receive him very coldly. I won't listen to any excuse from him."

Miss Spaulding: "Oh, yes, you will, Ethel!"

Miss Reed: "No, I shall not. If he wishes me to listen he must begin by humbling himself in the dust — yes, the dust, Nettie! I won't take anything short of it. I insist that he shall realize that I have suffered."

Miss Spaulding: "Perhaps he has suffered too!"

Miss Reed : " Oh, *he* suffered ! "

Miss Spaulding : " You know that he was perfectly devoted to you."

Miss Reed : " He never said so."

Miss Spaulding : " Perhaps he didn't dare.'

Miss Reed : " He dared to be very insolent to me."

Miss Spaulding : " And you know you liked him very much."

Miss Reed : " I won't let you say that, Nettie Spaulding. I *didn't* like him. I respected and admired him; but I didn't *like* him. He will never come near me; but if he does he has to begin by — by — Let me see, what shall I make him begin by doing ? " She casts up her eyes for inspiration while she leans forward over the register. " Yes, I will ! He has got to begin by taking that money ! "

Miss Spaulding : " Ethel, you *wouldn't* put that affront upon a sensitive and high-spirited man ! "

Miss Reed : " Wouldn't I ? You wait and *see,* Miss Spaulding ! He shall take the money, and he shall sign a receipt for it. I'll draw up the receipt now, so as to have it ready, and I shall ask him to sign it the very moment he enters this door — the very instant!" She takes a portfolio from the table near her, without rising, and writes: "'Received from Miss Ethel Reed one hundred and twenty-five dollars, in full, for twenty-five lessons in oil-painting.' There — when Mr. Oliver Ransom has signed this little document he may begin to talk; not before!" She leans back in her chair with an air of pitiless determination.

Miss Spaulding: "But, Ethel, you don't mean to make him take money for the lessons he gave you after he told you you couldn't learn anything?"

Miss Reed, after a moment's pause: "Yes, I do. This is to punish him. I don't wish for justice now; I wish for vengeance! At first I would have compromised on the six lessons, or on none at all, if he had behaved nicely; but after what's happened I shall insist upon paying him for every lesson, so as to make him feel that the whole thing, from first to last, was a purely business transaction on my part. Yes, a *purely* — BUSINESS — TRANSACTION!"

Miss Spaulding, turning to her music: "Then I've got nothing more to say to you, Ethel Reed."

Miss Reed: "I don't say but what, after he's taken the money and signed the receipt, I'll listen to anything else he's got to say, very willingly." *Miss Spaulding* makes no answer, but begins to play with a scientific absorption, feeling her way fitfully through the new piece, while *Miss Reed,* seated by the register, trifles with the book she has taken from the table.

II.

THE interior of the room of *Miss Spaulding* and *Miss Reed* remains in view, while the scene discloses, on the other side of the partition wall in the same house, the bachelor apartment of *Mr. Samuel Grinnidge*. *Mr. Grinnidge* in his dressing-gown and slippers, with his pipe in his mouth, has the effect of having just come in; his friend *Mr. Oliver Ransom* stands at the window, staring out into the November weather.

Grinnidge: "How long have you been waiting here?"

Ransom: "Ten minutes — ten years. How should I know?"

Grinnidge: "Well, I don't know who else should. Get back to-day?"

Ransom: "Last night."

Grinnidge: "Well, take off your coat, and pull up to the register, and warm your poor feet." He puts his hand out over the register. "Confound it! somebody's got the register open in the next room! You see, one pipe comes up from the furnace and branches into a V just under the floor, and professes to heat both rooms. But it don't. There was a fellow in there last winter who used to get all my heat. Used to go out and leave his register open, and I'd come in here just before dinner and find this place as cold as a barn. We had a running fight of it all winter. The man who got his register open first in the morning got all the heat for the day, for it never turned the other way when it started in one direction. Used to almost suffocate — warm, muggy days — maintaining my rights. Some piano-pounder in there this winter, it seems. Hear? And she hasn't lost any time in learning the trick of the register. What kept you so late in the country?"

Ransom, after an absent-minded pause: "Grinnidge, I wish you would give me some advice."

Grinnidge: "You can have all you want of it at the market price."

Ransom: "I don't mean your legal advice."

Grinnidge: "I'm sorry. What have you been doing?"

Ransom: "I've been making an ass of myself."

Grinnidge : "Wasn't that rather superfluous ? "

Ransom : "If you please, yes. But now, if you're capable of listening to me without any further display of your cross-examination wit, I should like to tell you how it happened."

Grinnidge : " I will do my best to veil my brilliancy. Go on."

Ransom : "I went up to Ponkwasset early in September for the foliage."

Grinnidge : " And staid till late in October. There must have been a reason for that. What was *her* name ? Foliage ? "

Ransom, coming up to the corner of the chimney-piece, near which his friend sits, and talking to him directly over the register: "I think you'll have to get along without the name for the present. I'll tell you by and by." As *Mr. Ransom* pronounces these words, *Miss Reed,* on her side of the partition, lifts her head with a startled air, and, after a moment of vague circumspection, listens keenly. "But she *was* beautiful. She was a blonde, and she had the loveliest eyes — eyes, you know, that could be funny or tender, just as she chose — the kind of eyes I always liked." *Miss Reed* leads forward over the register. " She had one of those faces that always leave you in doubt whether they're laughing at you, and so keep you in wholesome subjection; but you feel certain that they're *good,* and that if they did hurt you by laughing at you, they'd look sorry for you afterward. When she walked you saw what an exquisite creature she was. It always made me mad to think I couldn't *paint* her walk."

Grinnidge: "I suppose you saw a good deal of her walk." .

Ransom: "Yes; we were off in the woods and fields half the time together." He takes a turn towards the window.

Miss Reed, suddenly shutting the register on her side: "Oh!"

Miss Spaulding, looking up from her music: "What is it, Ethel?"

Miss Reed: "Nothing, nothing; I — I — thought it was getting too warm. Go on, dear; don't let me interrupt you." After a moment of heroic self-denial she softly presses the register open with her foot.

Ransom, coming back to the register: "It all began in that way. I had the good fortune one day to rescue her from a — cow."

Miss Reed: "Oh, for shame!"

Miss Spaulding, desisting from her piano: "What *is* the matter?"

Miss Reed, clapping the register to: "This ridiculous book! But don't — don't mind me, Nettie." Breathlessly: "Go — go — on!" *Miss Spaulding* resumes, and again *Miss Reed* softly presses the register open.

Ransom, after a pause: "The cow was grazing, and had no more thought of hooking Miss" —

Miss Reed: "Oh, I didn't suppose he *would!* — Go on, Nettie, go on! The hero — *such* a goose!"

Ransom: "I drove her away with my camp-stool, and Miss — the young lady — was as grateful as if I had rescued her from a menagerie of wild animals. I walked home with her to the farm-house, and the trouble began at once." Pantomime of indignant protest and burlesque menace on the part of *Miss Reed.* "There wasn't another well woman in the house, except her friend Miss Spaulding, who was rather old and rather plain." He takes another turn to the window.

Miss Reed: "Oh!" She shuts the register, but instantly opens it again. "Louder, Nettie."

Miss Spaulding, in astonishment: "What?"

Miss Reed: "Did I speak? I didn't know it. I" —

Miss Spaulding, desisting from practice: "What is that strange, hollow, rumbling, mumbling kind of noise?"

Miss Reed, softly closing the register with her foot: "I don't hear any strange, hollow, rumbling, mumbling kind of noise. Do you hear it *now?*"

Miss Spaulding: "No. It was the Brighton whistle, probably."

Miss Reed: "Oh, very likely." As *Miss Spaulding* turns again to her practice *Miss Reed* re-opens the register and listens again. A little interval of silence ensues, while *Ransom* lights a cigarette.

Grinnidge: "So you sought opportunities of rescuing her from other cows?"

Ransom, returning: "That wasn't necessary. The young lady was so impressed by my behavior, that she asked if I would give her some lessons in the use of oil."

Grinnidge: "She thought if she knew how to paint pictures like yours she wouldn't need any one to drive the cows away."

Ransom: "Don't be farcical, Grinnidge. That sort of thing will do with some victim on the

witness-stand who can't help himself. Of course
I said I would, and we were off half the time
together, painting the loveliest and loneliest bits
around Ponkwasset. It all went on very well, till
one day I felt bound in conscience to tell her that I
didn't think she would ever learn to paint, and that
if she was serious about it she'd better drop it at
once, for she was wasting her time."

Grinnidge, getting up to fill his pipe : " That
was a pleasant thing to do."

Ransom : "I told her that if it amused her, to
keep on ; I would be only too glad to give her all
the hints I could, but that I oughtn't to encourage
her. She seemed a good deal hurt. I fancied at
the time that she thought I was tired of having
her with me so much."

Miss Reed : "Oh, *did* you, indeed ! " To *Miss
Spaulding*, who bends an astonished glance upon
her from the piano: "The man in this book is the
most *conceited* creature, Nettie. Play chords —
something very subdued — ah ! "

Miss Spaulding : "What *are* you talking about,
Ethel ? "

Ransom : "That was at night; but the next day
she came up smiling, and said that if I didn't mind

she would keep on — for amusement; she wasn't a bit discouraged."

Miss Reed: "Oh! — Go on, Nettie; don't let my outbursts interrupt you."

Ransom: "I used to fancy sometimes that she *was* a little sweet on me."

Miss Reed: "You wretch! — Oh, scales, Nettie! Play scales!"

Miss Spaulding: "Ethel Reed, are you crazy?"

Ransom, after a thoughtful moment: "Well, so it went on for the next seven or eight weeks. When we weren't sketching in the meadows, or on the mountain-side, or in the old punt on the pond, we were walking up and down the farmhouse piazza together. She used to read to me when I was at work. She had a heavenly voice, Grinnidge."

Miss Reed: "Oh, you silly, silly thing! — Really this book makes me sick, Nettie."

Ransom: "Well, the long and the short of it was, I was hit — *hard*, and I lost all courage. You know how I am, Grinnidge."

Miss Reed, softly: "Oh, poor fellow!"

Ransom: "So I let the time go by, and at the end I hadn't said anything."

Miss Reed: "No, sir! You *hadn't!*" *Miss Spaulding* gradually ceases to play, and fixes her attention wholly upon *Miss Reed*, who bends for-ward over the register with an intensely excited face.

Ransom: "Then something happened that made me glad, for twenty-four hours at least, that I hadn't spoken. She sent me the money for twenty-five lessons. Imagine how I felt, Grinnidge! What could I suppose but that she had been quietly biding her time, and storing up her resent-ment for my having told her she couldn't learn to paint, till she could pay me back with interest in one supreme insult?"

Miss Reed, in a low voice: "Oh, how could you think such a cruel, vulgar thing?" *Miss Spaul-ding* leaves the piano, and softly approaches her, where she has sunk on her knees beside the register.

Ransom: "It was tantamount to telling me that she had been amusing herself with me instead of my lessons. It remanded our whole association, which I had got to thinking so romantic, to the relation of teacher and pupil. It was a snub — a heartless, killing snub; and I couldn't see it in any other light." *Ransom* walks away to the window, and looks out.

Miss Reed, flinging herself backward from the register, and hiding her face in her hands : "Oh, it wasn't! it wasn't! it wasn't! *How* could you think so ? "

Miss Spaulding, rushing forward, and catching her friend in her arms : "What is the matter with you, Ethel Reed ? What are you doing here, over the register ? Are you trying to suffocate yourself ? Have you taken leave of your senses ? "

Grinnidge : "Our fair friend on the other side of the wall seems to be on the rampage."

Miss Spaulding, shutting the register with a violent clash : "Ugh ! how hot it is here ! "

Grinnidge : "Doesn't like your conversation, apparently."

Miss Reed, frantically pressing forward to open the register : "Oh, don't shut it, Nettie, dear ! If you do I shall die ! Do-o-n't shut the register ! "

Miss Spaulding : "Don't shut it ? Why, we've got all the heat of the furnace in the room now. Surely you don't want any more ? "

Miss Reed : "No, no ; not any more. But—

but — Oh, dear! what shall I do?" She still struggles in the embrace of her friend.

Grinnidge, remaining quietly at the register, while *Ransom* walks away to the window: "Well, what did you do?"

Miss Reed: "There, there! They're commencing again! *Do* open it, Nettie. I *will* have it open!" She wrenches herself free, and dashes the register open.

Grinnidge: "Ah, she's opened it again."

Miss Reed, in a stage-whisper: "That's the other one!"

Ransom, from the window: "Do? I'll tell you what I did."

Miss Reed: "That's Ol — Mr. Ransom. And, oh, I can't make out what he's saying! He must have gone away to the other side of the room — and it's at the most important point!"

Miss Spaulding, in an awful undertone: "Was *that* the hollow rumbling I heard? And have you been listening at the register to what they've been saying? O *Ethel!*"

Miss Reed: "I haven't been listening, exactly."

Miss Spaulding: "You have! You have been eavesdropping!"

Miss Reed: "Eavesdropping is listening through a key-hole, or around a corner. This is very different. Besides, it's Oliver, and he's been talking about *me*. Hark!" She clutches her friend's hand, where they have crouched upon the floor together, and pulls her forward to the register. "Oh, dear, how hot it is! I wish they would cut off the heat down below."

Grinnidge, smoking peacefully through the silence which his friend has absent-mindedly let follow upon his last words: "Well, you seem disposed to take your time about it."

Ransom: "About what? Oh, yes! Well"—

Miss Reed: "'Sh! Listen."

Miss Spaulding: "I won't listen! It's shameful: it's wicked! I don't see how you can do it, Ethel!" She remains, however, kneeling near the register, and she involuntarily inclines a little more toward it.

Ransom: "— It isn't a thing that I care to shout from the house-tops." He returns from the window to the chimney-piece. "I wrote the rudest kind of note, and sent back her letter and her money in it. She had said that she hoped our acquaintance was not to end with the summer, but that we might sometimes meet in Boston; and I answered that our acquaintance had ended already, and that I should be sorry to meet her anywhere again."

Grinnidge: "Well, if you wanted to make an ass of yourself, you did it pretty completely."

Miss Reed, whispering: "How witty he is! Those men are always so humorous with each other."

Ransom: "Yes; I didn't do it by halves."

Miss Reed, whispering: "Oh, *that's* funny, too!"

Grinnidge: "It didn't occur to you that she might feel bound to pay you for the first half-dozen, and was embarrassed how to offer to pay for them alone?"

Miss Reed: "How he *does* go to the heart of the matter!" She presses *Miss Spaulding's* hand in an ecstasy of approval.

Ransom: "Yes, it did — afterward."

Miss Reed, in a tender murmur: "Oh, *poor* Oliver!"

Ransom: "And it occurred to me that she was perfectly right in the whole affair."

Miss Reed: "Oh, how generous! how noble!"

Ransom: "I had had a thousand opportunities,

and I hadn't been man enough to tell her that I was in love with her."

Miss Reed : "How can he say it right out so bluntly ? But if it's true " —

Ransom : "I *couldn't* speak. I was afraid of putting an end to the affair — of frightening her — disgusting her."

Miss Reed : "Oh, how little they know us, Nettie ! "

Ransom : "She seemed so much above me in every way — so sensitive, so refined, so gentle, so good, so angelic ! "

Miss Reed : " There ! *Now* do you call it eavesdropping ? If listeners never hear any good of themselves, what do you say to that ? It proves that I haven't been listening."

Miss Spaulding : "'Sh ! They're saying something else."

Ransom : " But all that's neither here nor there. I can see now that under the circumstances she couldn't as a lady have acted otherwise than she did. She was forced to treat our whole acquaintance as a business matter, and I had forced her to do it."

Miss Reed : " You *had*, you poor thing ! "

Grinnidge : " Well, what do you intend to do about it ? "

Ransom : " Well " —

Miss Reed : " 'Sh ! "

Miss Spaulding : " 'Sh ! "

Ransom : " — that's what I want to submit to you, Grinnidge. I must see her."

Grinnidge : " Yes. I'm glad *I* mustn't."

Miss Reed, stifling a laugh on *Miss Spaulding's* shoulder : " They're actually *afraid* of us, Nettie ! "

Ransom : " See her, and go down in the dust."

Miss Reed : " My very words ! "

Ransom : " I have been trying to think what was the very humblest pie I could eat, by way of penance ; and it appears to me that I had better begin by saying that I have come to ask her for the money I refused."

Miss Reed, enraptured : " Oh ! doesn't it seem just like — like — inspiration, Nettie ? "

Miss Spaulding : " 'Sh ! Be quiet, do ! You'll frighten them away ! "

Grinnidge : " And then what ? "

Ransom : " What then ? I don't know what then. But it appears to me that, as a gentleman, I've got nothing to do with the result. All that

I've got to do is to submit to my fate, whatever it is."

Miss Reed, breathlessly: "What princely courage! What delicate magnanimity! Oh, he needn't have the *least* fear! If I could only tell him that!"   •

Grinnidge, after an interval of meditative smoking : "Yes, I guess that's the best thing you can do. It will strike her fancy, if she's an imaginative girl, and she'll think you a fine fellow."

Miss Reed : "Oh, the horrid thing!"

Grinnidge : "If you humble yourself to a woman at all, do it thoroughly. If you go halfway down she'll be tempted to push you the rest of the way. If you flatten out at her feet to begin with, ten to one but she will pick you up."

Ransom : "Yes, that was my idea."

Miss Reed : "Oh, was it, indeed! Well!"

Ransom : "But I've nothing to do with her picking me up or pushing me down. All that I've got to do is to go and surrender myself."

Grinnidge : "Yes. Well; I guess you can't go too soon. I like your company ; but I advise you as a friend not to lose time. Where does she live ? "

Ransom: "That's the remarkable part of it: she lives in this house."

Miss Reed and *Miss Spaulding*, in subdued chorus: "Oh!"

Grinnidge, taking his pipe out of his mouth in astonishment: "No!"

Ransom: "I just came in here to give my good resolutions a rest while I was screwing my courage up to ask for her."

Miss Reed: "Don't you think he's *very* humorous? Give his good resolutions a rest! That's the way he *always* talks."

Miss Spaulding: "'Sh!"

Grinnidge: "You said you came for my advice."

Ransom: "So I did. But I didn't promise to act upon it. Well!" He goes toward the door.

Grinnidge, without troubling himself to rise: "Well, good luck to you!"

Miss Reed: "How droll they are with each other! Don't you *like* to hear them talk? Oh, I could listen all day."

Grinnidge, calling after *Ransom:* "You haven't told me your duck's name."

Miss Reed: "Is *that* what they call us? Duck!

Do you think it's very respectful, Nettie? I don't believe I like it. Or, yes, why not? It's no harm — if I *am* his duck!"

Ransom, coming back: "Well, I don't propose to go shouting it round. Her name is Miss Reed — Ethel Reed."

Miss Reed: "How *can* he?"

Grinnidge: "Slender, willowy party, with a lot of blond hair that looks as if it might be indigenous? Rather pensive-looking?"

Miss Reed: "Indigenous! I should hope so!"

Ransom: "Yes. But she isn't pensive. She's awfully deep. It makes me shudder to think how deep that girl is. And when I think of my courage in daring to be in love with her — a stupid, straightforward idiot like me — I begin to respect myself in spite of being such an ass. Well, I'm off. If I stay any longer I shall never go." He closes the door after him, and *Miss Reed* instantly springs to her feet.

Miss Reed: "Now he'll have to go down to the parlor and send up his name, and that just gives me time to do the necessary prinking. You stay here and receive him, Nettie."

Miss Spaulding: "Never! After what's happened I can never look him in the face again. Oh, how low, and mean, and guilty I feel!"

Miss Reed, with surprise: "Why, how droll! Now *I* don't feel the least so."

Miss Spaulding: "Oh, it's very different with *you.* You're in love with him."

Miss Reed: "For shame, Nettie! I'm *not* in love with him."

Miss Spaulding: "And you can explain and justify it. But I never can justify it to myself, much less to him. Let me go, Ethel! I shall tell Mrs. McKnight that we must change this room instantly. And just after I'd got it so nearly in order! Go down and receive him in the parlor, Ethel. I *can't* see him."

Miss Reed: "Receive him in the parlor! Why, Nettie, dear, you're crazy! I'm going to *accept* him: and how can I accept him — with all the consequences — in a public parlor? No, indeed! If you won't meet him here for a moment, just to oblige me, you can go into the other room. Or, no — you'd be listening to every word through the key-hole, you're so demoralized!"

Miss Spaulding: "Yes, yes, I deserve your con-tempt, Ethel."

Miss Reed, laughing: "You will have to go out for a walk, you poor thing; and I'm not going to have you coming back in five or ten minutes. You have got to stay out a good hour."

Miss Spaulding, running to get her things from the next room: "Oh, I'll stay out till midnight!"

Miss Reed, responding to a tap at the door: "Ye-e-s! Come in!—You're caught, Nettie."

A maid-servant, appearing with a card: "This gentleman is asking for you in the parlor, Miss Reed."

Miss Reed: "Oh! Ask him to come up here, please.—Nettie! Nettie!" She calls to her friend in the next room. "He's coming right up, and if you don't run you're trapped."

Miss Spaulding, re-appearing, cloaked and bonneted: "I don't blame *you*, Ethel, comparatively speaking. You can say that everything is fair in love. He will like it, and laugh at it in you, because he'll like everything you've done. Besides, you've no principles, and I *have*."

Miss Reed: "Oh, I've lots of principles, Nettie, but I've no practice!"

Miss Spaulding: "No matter. There's no excuse for me. I listened simply because I was a woman, and couldn't help it; and, oh, what will he think of me ? "

Miss Reed : "I won't give you away; if you really feel so badly " —

Miss Spaulding : "Oh, *do* you think you can keep from telling him, Ethel dear ? Try! And I will be your slave forever ! " Steps are heard on the stairs outside. "Oh, there he comes ! " She dashes out of the door, and closes it after her, a moment before the maid-servant, followed by *Mr. Ransom,* taps at it.

III.

SCENE: *Miss Reed* opens the door, and receives *Mr. Ransom* with well-affected surprise and state, suffering him to stand awkwardly on the threshold for a moment.

She, coldly: "Oh!—Mr. Ransom!"

He, abruptly: "I've come"—

She: "Won't you come in?"

He, advancing a few paces into the room: "I've come"—

She, indicating a chair: "Will you sit down?"

He: "I must stand for the present. I've come to ask you for that money, Miss Reed, which I refused yesterday, in terms that I blush to think of. I was altogether and wholly in the wrong, and I'm ready to offer any imaginable apology or reparation. I'm ready to take the money and to sign a receipt, and then to be dismissed with whatever ignominy you please. I deserve anything—everything!"

She : "The money ?   Excuse me ; I don't know — I'm afraid that I'm not prepared to pay you the whole sum to-day."

He, hastily : "Oh, no matter! no matter!   I don't care for the money now.   I merely wish to — to assure you that I thought you were perfectly right in offering it, and to — to " —

She : " What ? "

He : "Nothing.   That is — ah — ah " —

She : "It's extremely embarrassing to have people refuse their money when it's offered them, and then come the next day for it, when perhaps it isn't so convenient to pay it — *very* embarrassing."

He, hotly : "But I tell you I don't want the *money !*   I never wanted it, and wouldn't take it on any account."

She : "Oh!   I thought you said you came to get it ? "

He : " I said — I didn't say — I meant — that is — ah — I " —   He stops, open-mouthed.

She, quietly : " I could give you part of the money now."

He : "Oh, whatever you like ; it's indifferent " —

She : " Please sit down while I write a receipt." She places herself deliberately at the table, and opens her portfolio. "I will pay you now, Mr. Ransom, for the first six lessons you gave me — the ones before you told me that I could never learn to do anything."

He, sinking mechanically into the chair she indicates : "Oh, just as you like!" He looks up at the ceiling in hopeless bewilderment, while she writes.

She, blotting the paper : "There! And now let me offer you a little piece of advice, Mr. Ransom, which may be useful to you in taking pupils hereafter."

He, bursting out : "I never take pupils!"

She : "Never take pupils! I don't understand. You took *me.*"

He, confusedly : "I took you — yes. You seemed to wish — you seemed — the case was peculiar — peculiar circumstances."

She, with severity : "May I ask *why* the circumstances were peculiar? I saw nothing peculiar about the circumstances. It seemed to me it was a very simple matter. I told you that I had always had a great curiosity to see whether I could use oil paints, and I asked you a very plain question, whether you would let me study with you. Didn't I?"

He: "Yes."

She: "Was there anything wrong — anything queer about my asking you?"

He: No, no! Not at all — not in the least."

She: "Didn't you wish me to take the lessons of you? If you didn't, it wasn't kind of you to let me."

He: "Oh, I was perfectly willing — very glad indeed, very much so — certainly!"

She: "If it wasn't your *custom* to take pupils, you ought to have told me, and I wouldn't have forced myself upon you."

He, desperately: "It wasn't forcing yourself upon me. The Lord knows how humbly grateful I was. It was like a hope of heaven!"

She: "Really, Mr. Ransom, this is very strange talk. What am I. to understand by it? *Why* should you be grateful to teach me? Why should giving me lessons be like a hope of heaven?"

He: "Oh, I will tell you!"

She: "Well?"

He, after a moment of agony: "Because to be with you" —

She: "Yes?"

He: "Because I wished to be with you. Because — those days in the woods, when you read, and I " —

She : " Painted on my pictures " —

He : " Were the happiest of my life. Because — I loved you ! "

She : " Mr. Ransom ! "

He : " Yes, I must tell you so. I loved you; I love you still. I shall always love you, no matter what " —

She : " You forget yourself, Mr. Ransom. Has there been anything in my manner — conduct — to justify you in using such language to me ? "

He : " No — no " —

She : " Did you suppose that because I first took lessons of you from — from — an enthusiasm for art, and then continued them for — for — amusement, that I wished you to make love to me ? "

He : " No, I never supposed such a thing. I'm incapable of it. I beseech you to believe that no one could have more respect — reverence "— He twirls his hat between his hands, and casts an imploring glance at her.

She : " Oh, respect — reverence ! I know what they mean in the mouths of men. If you respected, if you reverenced me, could you dare to tell me, after my unguarded trust of you during the past months, that you had been all the time secretly in love with me?"

He, plucking up a little courage: "I don't see that the three things are incompatible."

She: "Oh, then you acknowledge that you did presume upon something you thought you saw in me to tell me that you loved me, and that you were in love with me all the time?"

He, contritely: "I have no right to suppose that you encouraged me; and yet—I can't deny it now—I was in love with you all the time."

She: "And you never said a word to let me believe that you had any such feeling toward me!"

He: "I—I"—

She: "You would have parted from me without a syllable to suggest it—perhaps parted from me forever?" After a pause of silent humiliation for him: "Do you call that brave or generous? Do you call it manly—supposing, as you hoped, that *I* had any such feeling?"

He: "No; it was cowardly, it was mean, it was unmanly. I see it now, but I will spend my life in repairing the wrong, if you will only let me."

He impetuously advances some paces toward her, and then stops, arrested by her irresponsive attitude.

She, with a light sigh, and looking down at the paper, which she has continued to hold between her hands: "There was a time — a moment — when I might have answered as you wish."

He: "Oh! then there will be again. If you have changed once, you may change once more. Let me hope that some time — any time, dearest "—

She, quenching him with a look: "Mr. Ransom, I shall *never* change toward you! You confess that you had your opportunity, and that you despised it."

He: "Oh! *not* despised it!"

She: "Neglected it."

He: "Not wilfully — no. I confess that I was stupidly, vilely, pusillan — pusillan — illani "—

She: "'Mously " —

He: "Thanks — 'mously unworthy of it; but I didn't despise it; I didn't neglect it; and if you will only let me show by a lifetime of devotion how dearly and truly I have loved you from the first moment I drove that cow away " —

She: "Mr. Ransom, I have told you that I

should never change toward you. That cow was nothing when weighed in the balance against your being willing to leave a poor girl, whom you supposed interested in you, and to whom you had paid the most marked attention, without a word to show her that you cared for her. What is a cow, or a whole herd of cows, as compared with obliging a young lady to offer you money that you hadn't earned, and then savagely flinging it back in her face ? A yoke of oxen would be nothing — or a mad bull."

He ! " Oh, I acknowledge it ! I confess it."

She : " And you own that I am right in refusing to listen to you now ? "

He, desolately : " Yes, yes."

She : " It seems that you gave me lessons in order to be with me, and if possible to interest me in you ; and then you were going away without a word."

He, with a groan : " It was only because I was afraid to speak."

She : " Oh, is *that* any excuse ? "

He : " No ; none."

She : " A man ought always to have courage." After a pause, in which he stands before her with bowed head: "Then there's nothing for me but to give you this money."

He, with sudden energy: "This is too much! I"—

She, offering him the bank-notes: "No; it is the exact sum. I counted it very carefully."

He: "I won't take it; I can't! I'll never take it!"

She, standing with the money in her outstretched hand: "I have your word as a gentleman that you will take it."

He, gasping: "Oh, well—I will take it—I will"—He clutches the money, and rushes toward the door. "Good-evening; ah—good-by"—

She, calling after him: "The receipt, Mr. Ransom! Please sign this receipt!" *She* waves the paper in the air.

He: "Oh, yes, certainly! Where is it—what—which"—*He* rushes back to her, and seizing the receipt, feels blindly about for the pen and ink. "Where shall I sign?"

She: "Read it first."

He: "Oh, it's all—all right"—

She: "I insist upon your reading it. It's a business transaction Read it aloud."

He, desperately : "Well, well!" *He* reads. "'Received from Miss Ethel Reed, in full, for twenty-five lessons in oil-painting, one hundred and twenty-five dollars, and her hand, heart, and dearest love forever.'" *He* looks up at her. "Ethel!"

She, smiling: "Sign it, sign it!"

He, catching her in his arms and kissing her: "Oh, yes — *here !* "

She, pulling a little away from him, and laughing : "Oh, oh! I only wanted *one* signature! Twenty autographs are too many, unless you'll let me trade them off, as the collectors do."

He : "No; keep them all! I couldn't think of letting any one else have them. One more!"

She : "No; it's quite enough!" *She* frees herself, and retires beyond the table. "This unexpected affection " —

He : " *Is* it unexpected — seriously ? "

She : "What do you mean ? "

He : " Oh, nothing ! "

She : "Yes, tell me ! "

He : "I hoped — I thought — perhaps — that you might have been prepared for some such demonstration on my part."

She: "And why did you think — hope — perhaps — *that,* Mr. Ransom, may I ask ?"

He: "If I hadn't, how should I have dared to speak ?"

She: "Dared ? You were obliged to speak ! Well, since it's all over, I don't mind saying that I *did* have some slight apprehensions that something in the way of a declaration might be extorted from you."

He: "Extorted ? Oh !" He makes an impassioned rush toward her.

She, keeping the table between them : "No, no."

He: "Oh, I merely wished to ask why you chose to make me suffer so, after I had come to the point."

She: "Ask it across the table, then." After a moment's reflection, "I made you suffer — I made you suffer — so that you might have a realizing sense of what you had made *me* suffer."

He, enraptured by this confession: "Oh, you angel !"

She, with tender magnanimity: "No; only a woman — a poor, trusting, foolish woman !" She permits him to surround the table, with imaginable results. Then, with her head on his shoulder :

" You'll *never* let me regret it, will you, darling ? You'll never oblige me to punish you again, dearest, will you ? Oh, it hurt *me* far worse to *see* your pain than it did you to — to — feel it ! " On the other side of the partition, *Mr. Grinnidge's* pipe falls from his lips, parted in slumber, and shivers to atoms on the register. " Oh ! " *She* flies at the register with a shriek of dismay, and is about to close it. " That wretch has been listening, and has heard every word ! "

He, preventing her : " What wretch ? Where ? "

She : " Don't you hear him, mumbling and grumbling there ? "

Grinnidge : " Well, I swear ! Cash value of twenty-five dollars, and untold toil in coloring it ! "

Ransom, listening with an air of mystification : " Who's that ? "

She : " Gummidge, Grimmidge — whatever you called him. Oh ! " *She* arrests herself in consternation. " Now I *have* done it ! "

He : " Done what ? "

She : " Oh — nothing ! "

He : " I don't understand. Do you mean to say that my friend Grinnidge's room is on the other side of the wall, and that you can hear him talk through the register?" *She* preserves the silence of abject terror. He stoops over the register, and calls down it. "Grinnidge! Hallo!"

Grinnidge: "Hallo, yourself!"

Ransom, to *Miss Reed:* "Sounds like the ghostly squeak of the phonograph." To *Grinnidge:* "What's the trouble?"

Grinnidge: "Smashed my pipe. Dozed off and let it drop on this infernal register."

Ransom, turning from the register with impressive deliberation: "Miss Reed, may I ask *how* you came to know that his name was Gummidge, or Grimmidge, or whatever I called him?"

She: Oh, dearest, I *can't* tell you! Or — yes, I had better." Impulsively: "I will judge you by myself. *I* could forgive *you* anything!"

He, doubtfully: "Oh, could you?"

She: "Everything! I had — I had better make a clean breast of it. Yes, I had. Though I don't like to. I — I listened!"

He: "Listened?"

She: "Through the register to — to — what — you — were saying before you — came in here." Her head droops.

He: "Then you heard everything?"

She : "Kill me, but don't look *so* at me ! It was accidental at first — indeed it was ; and then I recognized your voice ; and then I knew you were talking about me ; and I had so much at stake ; and I did love you so dearly ! You *will* forgive me, darling ? It wasn't as if I were listening with any bad motive."

He, taking her in his arms : " Forgive you ? Of course I do. But you must change this room at once, Ethel ; you see you hear everything on the other side, too."

She : " Oh, not if you whisper on this. You couldn't hear *us ?* " At a dubious expression of his : " You *didn't* hear us ? If you did, I can never forgive you ! "

He : " It was accidental at first — indeed it was ; and then I recognized your voice ; and then I knew you were talking about me ; and I had so much at stake ; and I did love you so dearly ! "

She : " All that has nothing whatever to do with it. How much did you hear ? "

He, with exemplary meekness : " Only what you were saying before Grinnidge came in. You didn't whisper then. I had to wait there for him while " —

She : " While you were giving your good resolutions a rest ? "

He : " While I was giving my good resolutions a rest."

She : " And that accounts for your determination to humble yourself so ? "

He : " It seemed perfectly providential that I should have known just what conditions you were going to exact of me."

She : " Oh, don't make light of it ! I can tell you it's a very serious matter."

He : " It was very serious for me when you didn't meet my self-abasement as you had led me to expect you would."

She : " Don't make fun ! I'm trying to think whether I can forgive you."

He, with insinuation : " Don't you believe you could think better if you put your head on my shoulder ? "

She : " Nonsense ! Then I should forgive you without thinking." After a season of reflection : " No, I *can't* forgive you. I never could forgive eavesdropping. It's *too* low."

He, in astonishment: " Why, you did it yourself ! "

She: "But you began it. Besides, it's very different for a man. Women are weak, poor, helpless creatures. They have to use finesse. But a man should be above it."

He: " You said you could forgive me anything."

She: " Ah, but I didn't know what you'd been doing ! "

He, with pensive resignation, and a feint of going : " Then I suppose it's all over between us."

She, relenting : " If you could think of any reason *why* I should forgive you " —

He: " I can't."

She, after consideration : " Do you suppose Mr. Grumage, or Grimidge, heard too ? "

He: "No ; Grinnidge is a very high-principled fellow, and wouldn't listen ; besides, he wasn't there, you know."

She: " Well, then, I will forgive you on these grounds." *He* instantly catches her to his heart. "But these alone, remember."

He, rapturously : " Oh, on any ! "

She, tenderly : " And you'll always be devoted ? And nice ? And not try to provoke me ? Or neglect me ? Or anything ? "

He: " Always ! Never ! "

She : " Oh, you dear, sweet, simple old thing — how I *do* love you ! "

Grinnidge, who has been listening attentively to every word at the register at his side : " Ransom, if you don't want me to go stark mad, *shut the register !* "

Ransom, about to comply : " Oh, poor old man ! I forgot it was open ! "

Miss Reed, preventing him : " No ! If he has been vile enough to listen at a register, let him suffer. Come, sit down here, and I'll tell you just when I began to care for you. It was long before the cow. Do you remember that first morning after you arrived " — *She* drags him close to the register, so that every word may tell upon the envious Grinnidge, on whose manifestations of acute despair, a rapid curtain descends.

THE ELEVATOR.

FARCE.

THE ELEVATOR.

Farce.

I.

SCENE: Through the curtained doorway of *Mrs. Edward Roberts's* pretty drawing-room, in Hotel Bellingham, shows the snowy and gleaming array of a table set for dinner, under the dim light of gas-burners turned low. An air of expectancy pervades the place, and the uneasiness of *Mr. Roberts*, in evening dress, expresses something more as he turns from a glance into the dining-room, and still holding the *portière* with one hand, takes out his watch with the other.

Mr. Roberts to *Mrs. Roberts* entering the drawing-room from regions beyond: "My dear, it's six o'clock. What can have become of your aunt?"

Mrs. Roberts, with a little anxiety: "That was just what I was going to ask. She's never late; and the children are quite heart-broken. They

161

had counted upon seeing her, and talking Christmas a little before they were put to bed."

Roberts : "Very singular her not coming! Is she going to begin standing upon ceremony with us, and not come till the hour ? "

Mrs. Roberts : "Nonsense, Edward! She's been detained. Of course she'll be here in a moment. How impatient you are ! "

Roberts : " You must profit by me as an awful example."

Mrs. Roberts, going about the room, and bestowing little touches here and there on its ornaments : "If you'd had that new cook to battle with over this dinner, you'd have learned patience by this time without any awful example."

Roberts, dropping nervously into the nearest chair: "I hope she isn't behind time."

Mrs. Roberts, drifting upon the sofa, and disposing her train effectively on the carpet around her : " She's before time. The dinner is in the last moment of ripe perfection now, when we must still give people fifteen minutes' grace." She studies the convolutions of her train absentmindedly.

Roberts, joining in its perusal: "Is that the

way you've arranged to be sitting when people come in ? "

Mrs. Roberts: "Of course not. I shall get up to receive them."

Roberts: "That's rather a pity. To destroy such a lovely pose."

Mrs. Roberts: "Do you like it ? "

Roberts: "It's divine."

Mrs. Roberts: "You might throw me a kiss."

Roberts: "No; if it happened to strike on that train anywhere, it might spoil one of the folds. I can't risk it." A ring is heard at the apartment door. They spring to their feet simultaneously.

Mrs. Roberts: "There's Aunt Mary now ! " She calls into the vestibule, "Aunt Mary ! "

Dr. Lawton, putting aside the vestibule *portière,* with affected timidity: "Very sorry. Merely a father."

Mrs. Roberts: "Oh ! Dr. Lawton ? I am so glad to see you ! " She gives him her hand : "I thought it was my aunt. We can't understand why she hasn't come. Why ! where's Miss Lawton ? "

Lawton: "That is precisely what I was going to ask you."

Mrs. Roberts : "Why, she isn't here."

Lawton : "So it seems. I left her with the carriage at the door when I started to walk here. She called after me down the stairs that she would be ready in three seconds, and begged me to hurry, so that we could come in together, and not let people know I'd saved half a dollar by walking."

Mrs. Roberts : "*She's* been detained too ! "

Roberts, coming forward : "Now you know what it is to have a delinquent Aunt-Mary-in-law."

Lawton, shaking hands with him : "O Roberts! Is that you ? It's astonishing how little one makes of the husband of a lady who gives a dinner. In my time — a long time ago — he used to carve. But nowadays, when everything is served *à la Russe,* he might as well be abolished. Don't you think, on the whole, Roberts, you'd better not have come ? "

Roberts : "Well, you see, I had no excuse. I hated to say an engagement when I hadn't any."

Lawton : "Oh, I understand. You *wanted* to come. We all do, when Mrs. Roberts will let us." He goes and sits down by *Mrs. Roberts,* who has taken a more provisional pose on the sofa.

"Mrs. Roberts, you're the only woman in Boston who could hope to get people, with a fireside of their own — or a register — out to a Christmas dinner. You know I still wonder at your effrontery a little?"

Mrs. Roberts, laughing: "I knew I should catch you if I baited my hook with your old friend."

Lawton : "Yes, nothing would have kept me away when I heard Bemis was coming. But he doesn't seem so inflexible in regard to me. Where is he?"

Mrs. Roberts : "I'm sure I don't know. I'd no idea I was giving such a formal dinner. But everybody, beginning with my own aunt, seems to think it a ceremonious occasion. There are only to be twelve. Do you know the Millers?"

Lawton : "No, thank goodness! One meets some people so often that one fancies one's weariness of them reflected in their sympathetic countenances. Who are these acceptably novel Millers?"

Mrs. Roberts : "Do explain the Millers to the doctor, Edward."

Roberts, standing on the hearth-rug, with his thumbs in his waistcoat pockets: "They board."

Lawton : "Genus. That accounts for their willingness to flutter round your evening lamp when they ought to be singeing their wings at their own. Well, species ? "

Roberts: "They're very nice young newly married people. He's something or other of some kind of manufactures. And Mrs. Miller is disposed to think that all the other ladies are as fond of him as she is."

Mrs. Roberts: "Oh! That is not so, Edward."

Lawton: "You defend your sex, as women always do. But you'll admit that, as your friend, Mrs. Miller may have this foible."

Mrs. Roberts: "I admit nothing of the kind. And we've invited another young couple who haven't gone to housekeeping yet — the Curwens. And *he* has the same foible as Mrs. Miller." *Mrs. Roberts* takes out her handkerchief, and laughs into it.

Lawton: "That is, if Mrs. Miller has it, which we both deny. Let us hope that Mrs. Miller and Mr. Curwen may not get to making eyes at each other."

Roberts: "And Mr. Bemis and his son complete the list. Why, Agnes, there are only ten. You said there were twelve."

Mrs. Roberts : "Well, never mind. I meant ten. I forgot that the Somerses declined." A ring is heard. "Ah! *that's* Aunt Mary." She runs into the vestibule, and is heard exclaiming without: "Why, Mrs. Miller, is it you? I thought it was my aunt. Where is Mr. Miller?"

Mrs. Miller, entering the drawing-room arm in arm with her hostess: "Oh, he'll be here directly. I had to let him run back for my fan."

Mrs. Roberts : "Well, we're very glad to have you to begin with. Let me introduce Dr. Lawton."

Mrs. Miller, in a polite murmur: " Dr. Lawton." In a louder tone: "O Mr. Roberts!"

Lawton : "You see, Roberts? The same aggrieved surprise at meeting you here that I felt."

Mrs. Miller : "What in the world do you mean ? "

Lawton : "Don't you think that when a husband is present at his wife's dinner party he repeats the mortifying superfluity of a bridegroom at a wedding ? "

Mrs. Miller : "I'm *sure* I don't know what you mean. I should never think of giving a dinner without Mr. Miller."

Lawton: "No?" A ring is heard. "There's Bemis."

Mrs. Miller: "It's Mr. Miller."

Mrs. Roberts: "Aunt Mary at last!" As she bustles toward the door: "Edward, there *are* twelve — Aunt Mary and Willis."

Roberts: "Oh, yes. I totally forgot Willis."

Lawton: "Who's Willis?"

Roberts: "Willis? Oh, Willis is my wife's brother. We always have him."

Lawton: "Oh, yes, Campbell."

Mrs. Roberts, without: "Mr. Bemis! So kind of you to come on Christmas."

Mr. Bemis, without: "So kind of you to ask us houseless strangers."

Mrs. Roberts, without: "I ran out here, thinking it was my aunt. She's played us a trick, and hasn't come yet."

Bemis, entering the drawing-room with *Mrs. Roberts:* "I hope she won't fail altogether. I haven't met her for twenty years, and I counted so much upon the pleasure — Hello, Lawton!"

Lawton: "Hullo, old fellow!" They fly at each other, and shake hands. "Glad to see you again."

Bemis, reaching his left hand to *Mr. Roberts,* while *Mr. Lawton* keeps his right: "Ah! Mr. Roberts."

Lawton : "Oh, never mind *him.* He's merely the husband of the hostess."

Mrs. Miller, to *Roberts :* "What *does* he mean ? "

Roberts : "Oh, nothing. Merely a joke he's experimenting with."

Lawton to *Bemis :* "Where's your boy ? "

Bemis : "He'll be here directly. He preferred to walk. Where's your girl ? "

Lawton : "Oh, she'll come by and by. She preferred to drive."

Mrs. Roberts, introducing them: "Mr. Bemis, have you met Mrs. Miller ? " She drifts away again, manifestly too uneasy to resume even a provisional pose on the sofa, and walks detachedly about the room.

Bemis : "What a lovely apartment Mrs. Roberts has."

Mrs. Miller : "Exquisite ! But then she has such perfect taste."

Bemis, to *Mrs. Roberts,* who drifts near them: "We were talking about your apartment, Mrs. Roberts. It's charming."

Mrs. Roberts: "It *is* nice. It's the ideal way of living. All on one floor. No stairs. Nothing."

Bemis: "Yes, when once you get here! But that little matter of five pair up" —

Mrs. Roberts: "You don't mean to say you *walked* up! Why in the world didn't you take the elevator?"

Bemis: "I didn't know you had one."

Mrs. Roberts: "It's the only thing that makes life worth living in a flat. All these apartment hotels have them."

Bemis: "Bless me! Well, you see, I've been away from Boston so long, and am back so short a time, that I can't realize your luxuries and conveniences. In Florence we *always* walk up. They have *ascenseurs* in a few great hotels, and they brag of it in immense signs on the sides of the building."

Lawton: "What pastoral simplicity! We are elevated here to a degree that you can't conceive of, gentle shepherd. Has yours got an air-cushion, Mrs. Roberts?"

Mrs. Roberts: "An air-cushion? What's that?"

Lawton: "The only thing that makes your life worth a moment's purchase in an elevator. You get in with a glass of water, a basket of eggs, and a file of the 'Daily Advertiser.' They cut the elevator loose at the top, and you drop."

Both Ladies : " Oh ! "

Lawton : "In three seconds you arrive at the ground-floor, reading your file of the ' Daily Advertiser ; ' not an egg broken nor a drop spilled. I saw it done in a New York hotel. The air is compressed under the elevator, and acts as a sort of ethereal buffer."

Mrs. Roberts : " And why don't we always go down in that way ? "

Lawton : " Because sometimes the walls of the elevator shaft give out."

Mrs. Roberts : " And what then ? "

Lawton : " Then the elevator stops more abruptly. I had a friend who tried it when this happened."

Mrs. Roberts : " And what did he do ? "

Lawton : " Stepped out of the elevator ; laughed ; cried ; went home ; got into bed : and did not get up for six weeks. Nervous shock. He was fortunate."

Mrs. Miller : " I shouldn't think you'd want an air-cushion on *your* elevator, Mrs. Roberts."

Mrs. Roberts : " No, indeed ! Horrid ! " The

bell rings. "Edward, *you* go and see if that's Aunt Mary."

Mrs. Miller: "It's Mr. Miller, I know."

Bemis: "Or my son."

Lawton: "My voice is for Mrs. Roberts's brother. I've given up all hopes of my daughter."

Roberts, without: "Oh, Curwen! Glad to see you! Thought you were my wife's aunt."

Lawton, at a suppressed sigh from *Mrs. Roberts:* "It's one of his jokes, Mrs. Roberts. Of course it's your aunt."

Mrs. Roberts, through her set teeth, smilingly: "Oh, if it *is,* I'll make him suffer for it."

Mr. Curwen, without: "No, I hated to wait, so I walked up."

Lawton: "It is Mr. Curwen, after all, Mrs. Roberts. Now let me see how a lady transmutes a frown of threatened vengeance into a smile of society welcome."

Mrs. Roberts: "Well, look!" To *Mr. Curwen,* who enters, followed by her husband: "Ah, Mr. Curwen! So glad to see you. You know all our friends here — Mrs. Miller, Dr. Lawton, and Mr. Bemis?"

Curwen, smiling and bowing, and shaking hands

right and left: "Very glad — very happy —
pleased to know you."

Mrs. Roberts, behind her fan to *Dr. Lawton:*
"Didn't I do it beautifully?"

Lawton, behind his hand : "Wonderfully! And
so unconscious of the fact that he hasn't his wife
with him."

Mrs. Roberts, in great astonishment, to *Mr.
Curwen:* "Where in the world is Mrs. Curwen?"

Curwen: "Oh — oh — she'll be here. I thought
she *was* here. She started from home with two
right-hand gloves, and I had to go back for a left,
and I — I suppose — Good heavens!" pulling
the glove out of his pocket. "I ought to have
sent it to her in the ladies' dressing-room." He
remains with the glove held up before him, in
spectacular stupefaction.

Lawton: "Only imagine what Mrs. Curwen
would be saying of you if she *were* in the dressing-room."

Roberts: "Mr. Curwen felt so sure she was
there that he wouldn't wait to take the elevator,
and walked up." Another ring is heard. "Shall
I go and meet your aunt *now*, my dear?"

Mrs. Roberts: "No, indeed! She may come in

now with all the formality she chooses, and I will receive her excuses in state." She waves her fan softly to and fro, concealing a murmur of trepida-tion under an indignant air, till the *portière* opens, and *Mr. Willis Campbell* enters. Then *Mrs. Roberts* breaks in nervous agitation "Why, Willis! Where's Aunt Mary?"

Mrs. Miller: "And Mr. Miller?"

Curwen: "And Mrs. Curwen?"

Lawton: "And my daughter?"

Bemis: "And my son?"

Mr. Campbell, looking tranquilly round on the faces of his interrogators: "Is it a conundrum?"

Mrs. Roberts, mingling a real distress with an effort of mock-heroic solemnity: "It is a tragedy! O Willis dear! it's what you see —what you hear; a niece without an aunt, a wife without a husband, a father without a son, and another father with-out a daughter."

Roberts: "And a dinner getting cold, and a cook getting hot."

Lawton: "And you are expected to account for the whole situation."

Campbell: "Oh, I understand! I don't know what your little game is, Agnes, but I can wait and see. *I'm* not hungry."

Mrs. Roberts: "Willis, do you think I would try and play a trick on you, if I could?"

Campbell: "I think you can't. Come, now, Agnes! It's a failure. Own up, and bring the rest of the company out of the next room. I suppose almost anything is allowable at this festive season, but this is pretty feeble."

Mrs. Roberts: "Indeed, indeed, they are not there."

Campbell: "Where are they, then?"

All: "That's what we don't know."

Campbell: "Oh, come, now! that's a little too thin. You don't know where *any* of all these blood-relations and connections by marriage are? Well, search me!"

Mrs. Roberts, in open distress: "Oh, I'm sure something must have happened to Aunt Mary!"

Mrs. Miller: "I can't understand what Ellery C. Miller means."

Lawton, with a simulated sternness: "I hope you haven't let that son of yours run away with my daughter, Bemis?"

Bemis: "I'm afraid he's come to a pass where he wouldn't ask *my* leave."

Curwen, re-assuring himself: "Ah, she's all right, of course. I know that" —

Bemis : " Miss Lawton ? "

Curwen : " No, no — Mrs. Curwen."

Campbell : " Is it a true bill, Agnes ? "

Mrs. Roberts : " Indeed it is, Willis. We've been expecting her for an hour — of course she always comes early — and I'm afraid she's been taken ill suddenly."

Roberts : " Oh, I don't think it's that, my dear."

Mrs. Roberts : " Oh, of course you never think anything's wrong, Edward. My whole family might die, and " — *Mrs. Roberts* restrains herself, and turns to *Mr. Campbell*, with hysterical cheerfulness : " Who came up in the elevator with you ? "

Campbell : " Me ? *I* didn't come in the elevator. I had my usual luck. The elevator was up somewhere, and after I'd pressed the annunciator button till my thumb ached, I watched my chance and walked up."

Mrs. Roberts : " Where was the janitor ? "

Campbell : " Where the janitor always is — nowhere."

Lawton : " Eating his Christmas dinner, probably."

Mrs. Roberts, partially abandoning and then recovering herself: " Yes, it's perfectly spoiled !

Well, friends, I think we'd better go to dinner —
that's the only way to bring them. I'll go out
and interview the cook." *Sotto voce* to her husband : " If I don't go somewhere and have a cry,
I shall break down here before everybody. Did
you ever know anything so strange ? It's perfectly — pokerish."

Lawton : " Yes, there's nothing like serving dinner to bring the belated guest. It's as infallible
as going without an umbrella when it won't rain."

Campbell : " No, no ! Wait a minute, Roberts.
You might sit down without one guest, but you
can't sit down without five. It's the old joke
about the part of Hamlet. I'll just step round to
Aunt Mary's house — why, I'll be back in three
minutes."

Mrs. Roberts, with perfervid gratitude : " Oh,
how *good* you are, Willis ! You don't know how
much you're doing ! What presence of mind you
have ! Why couldn't we have thought of sending
for her ? O Willis, I can never be grateful enough
to you ! But you always think of everything."

Roberts : " I accept my punishment meekly,
Willis, since it's in your honor."

Lawton : " It's a simple and beautiful solution,

Mrs. Roberts, as far as your aunt's concerned; but I don't see how it helps the rest of us."

Mrs. Miller to *Mr. Campbell:* "If you meet Mr. Miller " —

Curwen: "Or my wife " —

Bemis: "Or my son " —

Lawton: "Or my daughter " —

Campbell: "I'll tell them they've just one chance in a hundred to save their lives, and that one is open to them for just five minutes."

Lawton: "Tell my daughter that I've been here half an hour, and everybody knows I drove here with her."

Bemis: "Tell my son that the next time I'll walk, and let him drive."

Mrs. Miller: "Tell Mr. Miller I found I had my fan after all."

Curwen: "And Mrs. Curwen that I've got her glove all right."   He holds it up.

Mrs. Roberts, at a look of mystification and demand from her brother: "Never mind explanations, Willis. They'll understand, and we'll explain when you get back."

Lawton, examining the glove which *Curwen* holds up: "Why, so it *is* right!"

Curwen : " What do you mean ? "

Lawton : " Were you sent back to get a *left* glove ? "

Curwen : " Yes, yes ; of course."

Lawton : " Well, if you'll notice, this is a right one. The one at home is left."

Curwen, staring helplessly at it : " Gracious Powers ! what shall I do ? "

Lawton : " Pray that Mrs. Curwen may *never* come."

Mr. Curwen, dashing through the door : " I'll be back by the time Mr. Campbell returns."

Mrs. Miller, with tokens of breaking down visible to *Mrs. Roberts:* " I wonder what could have kept Mr. Miller. It's so very mysterious, I " —

Mrs. Roberts, suddenly seizing her by the arm, and hurrying her from the room : " Now, Mrs. Miller, you've just got time to see my baby."

Mr. Roberts, winking at his remaining guests : " A little cry will do them good. I saw as soon as Willis came in instead of her aunt, that my wife couldn't get through without it. They'll come back as bright as " —

Lawton : " Bemis, should you mind a bereaved father falling upon your neck ? "

Bemis: " Yes Lawton, I think I should."

Lawton: " Well, it *is* rather odd about all those people. You can say of one or two that they've been delayed, but five people can't have been delayed. It's too much. It amounts to a coincidence. Hello! What's that ? "

Roberts: " What's what ? "

Lawton: " I thought I heard a cry."

Roberts: " Very likely you did. They profess to deaden these floors so that you can't hear from one apartment to another. But I know pretty well when my neighbor overhead is trying to wheel his baby to sleep in a perambulator at three o'clock in the morning; and I guess our young lady lets the people below understand when she's wakeful. But it's the only way to live, after all. I wouldn't go back to the old up-and-down-stairs, house-in-a-block system on any account. Here we all live on the ground-floor practically. The elevator equalizes everything."

Bemis: " Yes, when it happens to be where you are. I believe I prefer the good old Florentine fashion of walking upstairs, after all."

Lawton: " Roberts, I *did* hear something Hark! It sounded like a cry for help. **There!** "

Roberts : " You're nervous, doctor. It's nothing. However, it's easy enough to go out and see." He goes out to the door of the apartment, and immediately returns. He beckons to *Dr. Lawton* and *Mr. Bemis,* with a mysterious whisper : "Come here both of you. Don't alarm the ladies."

II.

IN the interior of the elevator are seated *Mrs. Roberts's Aunt Mary (Mrs. Crashaw), Mrs. Curwen,* and *Miss Lawton; Mr. Miller* and *Mr. Alfred Bemis* are standing with their hats in their hands. They are in dinner costume, with their overcoats on their arms, and the ladies' draperies and ribbons show from under their outer wraps, where they are caught up, and held with that caution which characterizes ladies in sitting attitudes which they have not been able to choose deliberately. As they talk together, the elevator rises very slowly, and they continue talking for some time before they observe that it has stopped.

Mrs. Crashaw: "It's very fortunate that we are all here together. I ought to have been here half an hour ago, but I was kept at home by an accident to my finery, and before I could be put in repair I heard it striking the quarter past. I don't know what my niece will say to me. I hope you good people will all stand by me if she should be violent."

Miller: "In what a poor man may with his wife's fan, you shall command me, Mrs. Crashaw." He takes the fan out, and unfurls it.

Mrs. Crashaw: "Did she send you back for it?"

Miller: "I shouldn't have had the pleasure of arriving with you if she hadn't."

Mrs. Crashaw, laughing, to *Mrs. Curwen:* "What did you send *yours* back for, my dear?"

Mrs. Curwen, thrusting out one hand gloved, and the other ungloved: "I didn't want two rights."

Young Mr. Bemis: "Not even women's rights?"

Mrs. Curwen: "Oh, so young and so depraved! Are all the young men in Florence so bad?" Surveying her extended arms, which she turns over: "I don't know that I need have sent him for the other glove. I could have explained to Mrs. Roberts. Perhaps she would have forgiven my coming in one glove."

Miller, looking down at the pretty arms: "If she had seen you without."

Mrs. Curwen: "Oh, you were looking!" She rapidly involves her arms in her wrap. Then she suddenly unwraps them, and regards them thoughtfully. "What if he should bring a ten-button instead of an eight! And he's quite capable of doing it."

Miller: "Are there such things as ten-button gloves ?"

Mrs. Curwen: "You would think there were ten-thousand button gloves if you had them to button."

Miller: "It would depend upon whom I had to button them for."

Mrs. Curwen: "For Mrs. Miller, for example."

Mrs. Crashaw: "We women are too bad, always sending people back for something. It's well the men don't know *how* bad."

Mrs. Curwen: "'Sh! Mr. Miller is listening. And he thought we were perfect. He asks nothing better than to be sent back for his wife's fan. And he doesn't say anything even under his breath when she finds she's forgotten it, and begins, 'Oh, dearest, my fan'— Mr. Curwen does. But he goes all the same. I hope you have your father in good training, Miss Lawton. You must commence with your father, if you expect your husband to be 'good.'"

Miss Lawton: "Then mine will never behave, for papa is perfectly incorrigible."

Mrs. Curwen: "I'm sorry to hear such a bad report of him. ،Shouldn't *you* think he would be 'good,' Mr. Bemis?"

Young Mr. Bemis: "I should think he would try."

Mrs. Curwen: "A diplomat, as well as a punster already! I must warn Miss Lawton."

Mrs. Crashaw, interposing to spare the young people: "What an amusing thing elevator etiquette is! Why should the gentlemen take their hats off? Why don't you take your hats off in a horse-car?"

Miller: "The theory is that the elevator is a room."

Young Mr. Bemis: "We were at a hotel in London where they called it the Ascending Room."

Miss Lawton: "Oh, how amusing!"

Miller, looking about: "This is a regular drawing-room for size and luxury. They're usually such cribs in these hotels."

Mrs. Crashaw: "Yes, it's very nice, though I say it that shouldn't of my niece's elevator. The worst about it is, it's so slow."

Miller: "Let's hope it's sure."

Young Mr. Bemis: "Some of these elevators in America go up like express trains."

Mrs. Curwen, drawing her shawl about her shoulders, as if to be ready to step out: "Well, I never get into one without taking my life in my hand, and my heart in my mouth. I suppose every one really expects an elevator to drop with them, some day, just as everybody really expects to see a ghost some time."

Mrs. Crashaw: "Oh, my dear! what an extremely disagreeable subject of conversation."

Mrs. Curwen: "I can't help it, Mrs. Crashaw. When I reflect that there are two thousand elevators in Boston, and that the inspectors have just pronounced a hundred and seventy of them unsafe, I'm so desperate when I get into one that I could — flirt!"

Miller, guarding himself with the fan: "Not with me?"

Miss Lawton, to young *Mr. Bemis:* "How it *does* creep!"

Young Mr. Bemis, looking down fondly at her : " Oh, does it ? "

Mrs. Crashaw : " Why, it doesn't go at all ! It's stopped. Let us get out." They all rise.

The Elevator Boy, pulling at the rope : " We're not there, yet."

Mrs., Crashaw, with mingled trepidation and severity : " Not there ? What are you stopping, then, for ? "

The Elevator Boy : " I don't know. It seems to be caught."

Mrs. Crashaw : " Caught ? "

Miss Lawton : " Oh, dear ! "

Young Mr. Bemis : " Don't mind."

Miller : " Caught ? Nonsense ! "

Mrs. Curwen : " *We're* caught, I should say." She sinks back on the seat.

The Elevator Boy : " Seemed to be going kind of funny all day ! " He keeps tugging at the rope.

Miller, arresting the boy's efforts : " Well, hold on — stop ! What are you doing ? "

The Elevator Boy : " Trying to make it go."

Miller : " Well, don't be so — violent about it. You might break something."

The Elevator Boy : " Break a wire rope like that ! "

Miller: "Well, well, be quiet now. Ladies, I think you'd better sit down — and as gently as possible. I wouldn't move about much."

Mrs. Curwen: "Move! We're stone. And I wish for my part I were a feather."

Miller, to the boy: "Er — a — er — where do you suppose we are ? "

The Elevator Boy: "We're in the shaft between the fourth and fifth floors." He attempts a fresh demonstration on the rope, but is prevented.

Miller: "Hold on ! Er — er" —

Mrs. Crashaw, as if the boy had to .be communicated with through an interpreter: "Ask him if it's ever happened before."

Miller: "Yes. Were you ever caught before ? "

The Elevator Boy: "No."

Miller: "He says no."

Mrs. Crashaw: "Ask him if the elevator has a safety device."

Miller: "Has it got a safety device ? "

The Elevator Boy: "How should I know ? "

Miller: "He says he don't know."

Mrs. Curwen, in a shriek of hysterical laughter : " Why, he understands English ! "

Mrs. Crashaw, sternly ignoring the insinuation :

"Ask him if there's any means of calling the janitor."

Miller : "Could you call the janitor ? "

The Elevator Boy, ironically : " Well, there ain't any telephone attachment."

Miller, solemnly : " No, he says there isn't."

Mrs. Crashaw, sinking back on the seat with resignation : " Well, I don't know what my niece will say."

Miss Lawton : "Poor papa ! "

Young Mr. Bemis, gathering one of her wandering hands into his : " Don't be frightened. I'm sure there's no danger."

The Elevator Boy, indignantly : " Why, she can't *drop.* The cogs in the runs won't let her ! "

All : "Oh ! "

Miller, with a sigh of relief: "I knew there must be something of the kind. Well, I wish my wife had her fan."

Mrs. Curwen : "And if I had my left glove I should be perfectly happy. Not that I know what the cogs in the runs are ! "

Mrs. Crashaw : "Then we're merely caught here ? "

Miller : "That's all."

Mrs. Curwen: "It's quite enough for the purpose. Couldn't you put on a life-preserver, Mr. Miller, and go ashore and get help from the natives?"

Miss Lawton, putting her handkerchief to her eyes: "Oh, dear!"

Mrs. Crashaw, putting her arm around her: "Don't be frightened, my child. There's no danger."

Young Mr. Bemis, caressing the hand which he holds: "Don't be frightened."

Miss Lawton: "Don't leave me."

Young Mr. Bemis: "No, no; I won't. Keep fast hold of my hand."

Miss Lawton: "Oh, yes, I will! I'm ashamed to cry."

Young Mr. Bemis, fervently: "Oh, you needn't be! It is perfectly natural you should."

Mrs. Curwen: "I'm too badly scared for tears. Mr. Miller, you seem to be in charge of this expedition — couldn't you do something? Throw out ballast, or let the boy down in a parachute? Or I've read of a shipwreck where the survivors, in an open boat, joined in a cry, and attracted the notice of a vessel that was going to pass them. We might join in a cry."

Miller: "Oh, it's all very well joking, Mrs. Curwen " —

Mrs. Curwen: "You call it joking!"

Miller: "But it's not so amusing, being cooped up here indefinitely. I don't know how we're to get out. We can't join in a cry, and rouse the whole house. It would be ridiculous."

Mrs. Curwen: "And our present attitude is so eminently dignified! Well, I suppose we shall have to cast lots pretty soon to see which of us shall be sacrificed to nourish the survivors. It's long past dinner-time."

Miss Lawton, breaking down: "Oh, *don't* say such terrible things."

Young Mr. Bemis, indignantly comforting her: "Don't, don't cry. There's no danger. It's perfectly safe."

Miller to the Elevator Boy: "Couldn't you climb up the cable, and get on to the landing, and — ah! — get somebody?"

The Elevator Boy: "I could, maybe, if there was a hole in the roof."

Miller, glancing up: "Ah! true."

Mrs. Crashaw, with an old lady's serious kindness: "My boy, can't you think of anything to do for us?"

The Elevator Boy yielding to the touch of humanity, and bursting into tears: "No, ma'am, I can't. And everybody's blamin' me, as if I done it. What's my poor mother goin' to do?"

Mrs. Crashaw, soothingly: "But you said the runs in the cogs"—

The Elevator Boy: "How can I tell! That's what they say. They hain't never been tried."

Mrs. Curwen, springing to her feet: "There! I knew I should. Oh"—She sinks fainting to the floor.

Mrs. Crashaw, abandoning *Miss Lawton* to the ministrations of young *Mr. Bemis*, while she kneels beside *Mrs. Curwen* and chafes her hand: "Oh, poor thing! I knew she was overwrought by the way she was keeping up. Give her air, Mr. Miller. Open a — Oh, there isn't any window!"

Miller, dropping on his knees, and fanning *Mrs. Curwen:* "There! there! Wake up, Mrs. Curwen, I didn't mean to scold you for joking. I didn't, indeed. I — I — I don't know what the deuce I'm up to." He gathers *Mrs. Curwen's* inanimate form in his arms, and fans her face where it lies on his shoulder. "I don't know what my wife would say if"—

Mrs. Crashaw : "She would say that you were doing your duty."

Miller, a little consoled: "Oh, do you think so? Well, perhaps."

Young Mr. Bemis : "Do you feel faint at all, Miss Lawton?"

Miss Lawton : "No, I think not. No, not if you say it's safe."

Young Mr. Bemis : "Oh, I'm sure it is!"

Miss Lawton, renewing her hold upon his hand: "Well, then! Perhaps I hurt you?"

Young Mr. Bemis : "No, no! You couldn't."

Miss Lawton : "How kind you are!"

Mrs. Curwen, opening her eyes: "Where" —

Miller, rapidly transferring her to *Mrs. Crashaw :* "Still in the elevator, Mrs. Curwen." Rising to his feet: "Something must be done. Perhaps we *had* better unite in a cry. It's ridiculous, of course. But it's the only thing we can do. Now, then! Hello!"

Miss Lawton : "Papa!"

Mrs. Crashaw : "Agne-e-e-s!"

Mrs. Curwen, faintly: "Walter!"

The Elevator Boy : "Say!"

Miller : "Oh, that won't do. All join in 'Hello!'"

All: "Hello!"

Miller: "Once more!"

All: "Hello!"

Miller: "*Once* more!"

All: "Hello!"

Miller: "Now wait a while." After an interval: "No, nobody coming." He takes out his watch. "We must repeat this cry at intervals of a half-minute. Now, then!" They all join in the cry, repeating it as *Mr. Miller* makes the signal with his lifted hand.

Miss Lawton: "Oh, it's no use!"

Mrs. Crashaw: "They don't hear."

Mrs. Curwen: "They *won't* hear."

Miller: "Now, then, three times!"

All: "Hello! hello! hello!"

III.

Roberts appears at the outer door of his apartment on the fifth floor. It opens upon a spacious landing, to which a wide staircase ascends at one side. At the other is seen the grated door to the shaft of the elevator. He peers about on all sides, and listens for a moment before he speaks.

Roberts : " Hello yourself."

Miller, invisibly from the shaft : " Is that you, Roberts ? "

Roberts : " Yes ; where in the world are you ? "

Miller : " In the elevator."

Mrs. Crashaw : " We're *all* here, Edward."

Roberts : " What ! You, Aunt Mary ! "

Mrs. Crashaw : " Yes. Didn't I say so ? "

Roberts : " Why don't you come up ? "

Miller : " We can't. The elevator has got stuck somehow."

Roberts: "Got stuck? Bless my soul! How did it happen? How long have you been there?"

Mrs. Curwen: "Since the world began!"

Miller: "What's the use asking how it happened? We don't know, and we don't care. What we want to do is to get out."

Roberts: "Yes, yes! Be careful!" He rises from his frog-like posture at the grating, and walks the landing in agitation. "Just hold on a minute!"

Miller: "Oh, *we* sha'n't stir."

Roberts: "I'll see what can be done."

Miller: "Well, see quick, please. We have plenty of time, but we don't want to lose any. Don't alarm Mrs. Miller, if you can help it."

Roberts: "No, no."

Mrs. Curwen: "You *may* alarm Mr. Curwen."

Roberts: "What! Are *you* there?"

Mrs. Curwen: "Here? I've been here all my life!"

Roberts: "Ha! ha! ha! That's right. We'll soon have you out. Keep up your spirits."

Mrs. Curwen: "But I'm *not* keeping them up."

Miss Lawton: "Tell papa I'm here too."

Roberts: "What! You too, Miss Lawton?"

Mrs. Crashaw: "Yes, and young Mr. Bemis. Didn't I *tell* you we were all here?"

Roberts: "I couldn't realize it. Well, wait a moment."

Mrs. Curwen: "Oh, you can trust us to wait."

Roberts, returning with *Dr. Lawton,* and *Mr. Bemis,* who join him in stooping around the grated door of the shaft: "They're just under here in the well of the elevator, midway between the two stories."

Lawton: "Ha! ha! ha! You don't say so."

Bemis: "Bless my heart! What are they doing there?"

Miller: "We're not doing anything."

Mrs. Curwen: "We're waiting for you to do something."

Miss Lawton: "Oh, papa!"

Lawton: "Don't be troubled, Lou, we'll soon have you out."

Young Mr. Bemis: "Don't be alarmed, sir. Miss Lawton is all right."

Miss Lawton: "Yes, I'm not frightened, papa."

Lawton: "Well, that's a great thing in cases of this kind. How did you happen to get there?"

Miller, indignantly: "How do you suppose? We came up in the elevator."

Lawton: "Well, why didn't you come the rest of the way?"

Miller: "The elevator wouldn't."

Lawton: "What seems to be the matter?"

Miller: "We don't know."

Lawton: "Have you tried to start it?"

Miller: "Well, I'll leave that to your imagination."

Lawton: "Well, be careful what you do. You might" —

Miller, interrupting: "Roberts, who's that talking?"

Roberts, coming forward politely: "Oh, excuse me! I forgot that you didn't know each other. Dr. Lawton, Mr. Miller." Introducing them.

Lawton: "Glad to know you."

Miller: "Very happy to make your acquaintance, and hope some day to see you. And now, if you have completed your diagnosis" —

Mrs. Curwen: "None of us have ever had it before, doctor; nor any of our families, so far as we know."

Lawton: "Ha! ha! ha! Very good! Well, just keep quiet. We'll have you all out of there presently."

Bemis : "Yes, remain perfectly still."

Roberts : "Yes, we'll have you out. Just wait."

Miller : "You seem to think we're going to run away. Why shouldn't we keep quiet? Do you suppose we're going to be very boisterous, shut up here like rats in a trap?"

Mrs. Curwen : "Or birds in a cage, if you want a more pleasing image."

Mrs. Crashaw : "How are you going to get us out, Edward?"

Roberts : "We don't know yet. But keep quiet" —

Miller : "Keep quiet! Great heavens! we're afraid to stir a finger. Now don't say 'keep quiet' any more, for we can't stand it."

Lawton : "He's in open rebellion. What are you going to do, Roberts?"

Roberts, rising and scratching his head: "Well, I don't know yet. We might break a hole in the roof."

Lawton : "Ah, I don't think that would do. Besides you'd have to get a carpenter."

Roberts : "That's true. And it would make a racket, and alarm the house" — staring desperately at the grated doorway of the shaft. "If I could only find an elevator man — an elevator builder! But of course they all live in the suburbs, and they're keeping Christmas, and it would take too long, anyway."

Bemis: "Hadn't you better send for the police? It seems to me it's a case for the authorities."

Lawton: "Ah, there speaks the Europeanized mind! They always leave the initiative to the authorities. Go out and sound the fire-alarm, Roberts. It's a case for the Fire Department."

Roberts: "Oh, it's all very well to joke, Dr. Lawton. Why don't you prescribe something?"

Lawton: "Surgical treatment seems to be indicated, and I'm merely a general practitioner."

Roberts: "If Willis were only here, he'd find some way out of it. Well, I'll have to go for help somewhere " —

Mrs. Roberts and *Mrs. Miller*, bursting upon the scene: "Oh, what is it?"

Lawton: "Ah, you needn't go for help, my dear fellow. It's come!"

Mrs. Roberts: "What are you all doing here, Edward?"

Mrs. Miller: "Oh, have you had any bad news of Mr. Miller?"

Mrs. Roberts : "Or Aunt Mary ? "

Miller, calling up: "Well, are you going to keep us here all night ? Why don't you do something ? "

Mrs. Miller : "Oh, what's that ? Oh, it's Mr. Miller ! Oh, where are you, Ellery ? "

Miller : "In the elevator."

Mrs. Miller : "Oh ! and where is the elevator ? Why don't you get out ? Oh" —

Miller : "It's caught, and we can't."

Mrs. Miller : "Caught ? Oh, then you will be killed — killed — killed ! And it's all my fault, sending you back after my fan, and I had it all the time in my own pocket; and it comes from my habit of giving it to you to carry in your overcoat pocket, because it's deep, and the fan can't break. And of course I never thought of my own pocket, and I never *should* have thought of it at all if Mr. Curwen hadn't been going back to get Mrs. Curwen's glove, for he'd brought another right after she'd sent him for a left, and we were all having such a laugh about it, and I just happened to put my hand on my pocket, and there I felt the fan. And oh, *what* shall I do ? "

Mrs. Miller utters these explanations and self-reproaches in a lamentable voice, while crouching close to the grated door to the elevator shaft, and clinging to its meshes.

Miller: "Well, well, it's all right. I've got you another fan, here. Don't be frightened."

Mrs. Roberts, wildly: "Where's Aunt Mary, Edward? Has Willis got back?" At a guilty look from her husband: "Edward! *don't* tell me that *she's* in that elevator! Don't do it, Edward! For your own sake don't. Don't tell me that your own child's mother's aunt is down there, suspended between heaven and earth like — like " —

Lawton: "The coffin of the Prophet."

Mrs. Roberts: "Yes. *Don't* tell me, Edward! Spare your child's mother, if you won't spare your wife!"

Mrs. Crashaw: "Agnes! don't be ridiculous. I'm here, and I never was more comfortable in my life."

Mrs. Roberts, calling down the grating: "Oh! Is it you, Aunt Mary?"

Mrs. Crashaw: "Of course it is!"

Mrs. Roberts: "You recognize my voice?"

Mrs. Crashaw: "I should hope so, indeed! Why shouldn't I?"

Mrs. Roberts: "And you know me? Agnes? Oh!"

Mrs. Crashaw: "Don't be a goose, Agnes."

Mrs. Roberts: "Oh, it *is* you, aunty. It *is!* Oh, I'm *so* glad! I'm *so* happy! But keep perfectly still, aunty dear, and we'll soon have you out. Think of baby, and don't give way."

Mrs. Crashaw: "I shall not, if the elevator doesn't, you may depend upon that."

Mrs. Roberts: "Oh, what courage you *do* have! But keep up your spirits! Mrs. Miller and I have just come from seeing baby. She's gone to sleep with all her little presents in her arms. The children did want to see you so much before they went to bed. But never mind that now, Aunt Mary. I'm only too thankful to have you at all!"

Mrs. Crashaw: "I wish you did have me! And if you will all stop talking and try some of you to do something, I shall be greatly obliged to you. It's worse than it was in the sleeping-car that night."

Mrs. Roberts: "Oh, do you remember it, Aunt Mary? Oh, how funny you are!" Turning heroically to her husband: "Now, Edward, dear, get them out. If it's necessary, get them out over my dead body. Anything! Only hurry. I will be calm; I will be patient. But you must act instantly. Oh, here comes Mr. Curwen!" *Mr. Curwen* mounts the stairs to the landing with every sign of exhaustion, as if he had made a very quick run to and from his house. "Oh, *he* will help — I know he will! Oh, Mr. Curwen, the elevator is caught just below here with my aunt in it and Mrs. Miller's husband" —

Lawton : "And my girl."

Bemis : "And my boy."

Mrs. Curwen, calling up : "And your wife!"

Curwen, horror-struck : "And my wife! Oh, heavenly powers! what are we going to do? How shall we get them out? Why don't they come up?"

All : "They can't."

Curwen : "Can't? Oh, my goodness!" He flies at the grating, and kicks and beats it.

Roberts : "Hold on! What's the use of that?"

Lawton : "You couldn't get at them if you beat the door down."

Bemis : "Certainly not." They lay hands upon him and restrain him.

.

Curwen, struggling: "Let me speak to my wife! Will you prevent a husband from speaking to his own wife?"

Mrs. Miller, in blind admiration of his frenzy: "Yes, that's just what I said. If some one had beaten the door in at once" —

Mrs. Roberts: "Oh, Edward, dear, let him speak to his wife." Tearfully: "Think if *I* were there!"

Roberts, releasing him: "He may speak to his wife all night. But he mustn't knock the house down."

Curwen, rushing at the grating: "Caroline! Can you hear me? Are you safe?"

Mrs. Curwen: "Perfectly. I had a little faint when we first stuck" —

Curwen: "Faint? Oh!"

Mrs. Curwen: "But I am all right now."

Curwen: "Well, that's right. Don't be frightened! There's no occasion for excitement. Keep perfectly calm and collected. It's the only way — What's that ringing?" The sound of an electric bell is heard within the elevator. It increases in fury.

Mrs. Roberts and *Mrs. Miller:* "Oh, isn't it dreadful?"

The Elevator Boy: "It's somebody on the ground-floor callin' the elevator!"

Curwen: "Well, never mind him. Don't pay the slightest attention to him. Let him go to the deuce! And, Caroline!"

Mrs. Curwen: "Yes?"

Curwen: "I — I — I've got your glove all right."

Mrs. Curwen: "Left, you mean, I hope?"

Curwen: "Yes, left, dearest! I *mean* left."

Mrs. Curwen: "Eight-button?"

Curwen: "Yes."

Mrs. Curwen: "Light drab?"

Curwen, pulling a light yellow glove from his pocket: "Oh!" He staggers away from the grating and stays himself against the wall, the mistaken glove dangling limply from his hand.

Roberts, Lawton, and *Bemis:* "Ah! ha! ha! ha!"

Mrs. Roberts: "Oh, for shame! to laugh at such a time!"

Mrs. Miller: "When it's a question of life and death. There! The ringing's stopped. What's that?" Steps are heard mounting the stairway rapidly, several treads at a time. *Mr. Campbell* suddenly bursts into the group on the landing with a final bound from the stairway. "Oh!"

Campbell: "I can't find Aunt Mary, Agnes. I can't find anything — not even the elevator. Where's the elevator? I rang for it down there till I was black in the face."

Mrs. Roberts: "No wonder! It's here."

Mrs. Miller: "Between this floor and the floor below. With my husband in it."

Curwen: "And my wife!"

Lawton: "And my daughter!"

Bemis: "And my son!"

Mrs. Roberts: "And aunty!"

All: "And it's stuck fast."

Roberts: "And the long and short of it is, Willis, that we don't know how to get them out, and we wish you would suggest some way."

Lawton: "There's been a great tacit confidence among us in your executive ability and your inventive genius."

Mrs. Roberts: "Oh, yes, we know you can do it."

Mrs. Miller: "If you can't, nothing can save them."

Campbell, going to the grating: "Miller!"

Miller: "Well?"

Campbell: "Start her up!"

Miller: "Now, look here, Campbell, we are not going to stand that; we've had enough of it. I speak for the whole elevator. Don't you suppose that if it had been possible to start her up we" —

Mrs. Curwen: "We shouldn't have been at the moon by this time."

Campbell: "Well, then, start her *down!*"

Miller: "I never thought of that." To the *Elevator Boy:* "Start her down." To the people on the landing above: "Hurrah! She's off!"

Campbell: "Well, *now* start her up!"

A joint cry from the elevator: "Thank you! we'll *walk* up this time."

Miller: "Here! let us out at this landing!" They are heard precipitately emerging, with sighs and groans of relief, on the floor below.

Mrs. Roberts, devoutly: "O Willis, it seems like an interposition of Providence, your coming just at this moment."

Campbell: "Interposition of common sense! These hydraulic elevators weaken sometimes, and can't go any farther."

Roberts, to the shipwrecked guests, who arrive

at the top of the stairs, crestfallen, spent, and clinging to one another for support: "Why didn't you think of starting her down, some of you?"

Mrs. Roberts, welcoming them with kisses and hand-shakes: "I should have thought it would occur to you at once."

Miller, goaded to exasperation: "Did it occur to any of *you?*"

Lawton, with sublime impudence: "It occurred to *all* of us. But we naturally supposed you had tried it."

Mrs. Miller, taking possession of her husband: "Oh, what a fright you have given us!"

Miller: "*I* given you! Do you suppose I did it out of a joke, or voluntarily?"

Mrs. Roberts: "Aunty, I don't know what to say to you. *You* ought to have been here long ago, before anything happened."

Mrs. Crashaw: "Oh, I can explain everything in due season. What I wish you to do now is to let me get at Willis, and kiss him." As *Campbell* submits to her embrace: "You dear, good fellow! If it hadn't been for your presence of mind, I don't know how we should ever have got out of that horrid pen."

Mrs. Curwen, giving him her hand: "As it isn't proper for *me* to kiss you " —

Campbell: "Well, I don't know. I don't wish to be *too* modest."

Mrs. Curwen: "I think I shall have to vote you a service of plate."

Mrs. Roberts: "Come and look at the pattern of mine. And, Willis, as you are the true hero of the occasion, you shall take me in to dinner. And I am not going to let anybody go before you." She seizes his arm, and leads the way from the landing into the apartment. *Roberts, Lawton,* and *Bemis* follow stragglingly.

Mrs. Miller, getting her husband to one side: "When she fainted, she fainted *at* you, of course! What did you do?"

Miller: "Who? I! Oh!" After a moment's reflection: "She came to!"

Curwen, getting his wife aside: "When you fainted, Caroline, who revived you?"

Mrs. Curwen: "Who? *Me?* Oh! How should I know? I was insensible." They wheel arm in arm, and meet *Mr.* and *Mrs. Miller* in the middle. *Mrs. Curwen* yields precedence with an ironical courtesy: "After you, Mrs. Miller!"

Mrs. Miller, in a nervous, inimical twitter : " Oh, before the heroine of the lost elevator ? "

Mrs. Curwen, dropping her husband's arm, and taking *Mrs. Miller's :* " Let us split the difference."

Mrs. Miller : " Delightful ! I shall never forget the honor."

Mrs. Curwen : " Oh, don't speak of honors ! Mr. Miller was *so* kind through all those terrible scenes in the elevator."

Mrs. Miller : " I've no doubt you showed yourself duly grateful." They pass in, followed by their husbands.

Young Mr. Bemis, timidly : " Miss Lawton, in the elevator you asked me not to leave you. Did you — ah — mean — I *must* ask you ; it may be my only chance ; if you meant — never ? "

Miss Lawton, dropping her head : " I — I — don't — know."

Young Mr. Bemis : " But if I *wished* never to leave you, should you send me away ? "

Miss Lawton, with a shy, sly upward glance at him : " Not in the elevator ! "

Young Mr. Bemis : " Oh ! "

Mrs. Roberts, re-appearing at the door : " Why,

you good-for-nothing young things, why don't you come to— Oh! excuse me!" She re-enters precipitately, followed by her tardy guests, on whom she casts a backward glance of sympathy. "Oh, you *needn't* hurry!"